EDEN

Book 2

Georgia Le Carre

ALSO BY GEORGIA

The Billionaire Banker Series

Owned
42 Days
Besotted
Seduce Me
Love's Sacrifice

Masquerade

Pretty Wicked
(Novella)

Disfigured Love

Eden

Click on the link below to receive news of my latest releases, fabulous giveaways, and exclusive content.
http://bit.ly/1Oe9WdE

Cover Designer: http://www.boomingcovers.blogspot.co.uk/
Editor: http://www.loriheaford.com/
Proofreader: http:// www.nicolarheadediting.com

EDEN

Book 2

Published by Georgia Le Carre
Copyright © 2015 by Georgia Le Carre

ISBN: 978-1-910575-07-9

You can discover more information about Georgia Le Carre
and future releases here.

https://www.facebook.com/georgia.lecarre
https://twitter.com/georgiaLeCarre
http://www.goodreads.com/GeorgiaLeCarre

ACKNOWLEDGEMENTS

Thank you so, so very much to SueBee, Caryl Milton, Elizabeth Burns, Shannon Komasincki, Nicola Rhead, Chelle Thompson, C.J Fallowfield, Nichole Hart, Cariad & Sandra Hayes for all your help. It is very much appreciated.

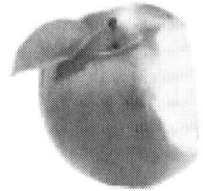

O Mother, I have made a bird of prey my lover,
When I give him bits of bread he doesn't eat,
So I feed him with the flesh of my heart.
—Shiv Kumar Batalvi

Contents

ONE 1

TWO 5

THREE 10

FOUR...17

FIVE 26

SIX 31

SEVEN...37

EIGHT 43

NINE 52

TEN 59

ELEVEN...70

TWELVE 77

THIRTEEN 85

FOURTEEN 91

FIFTEEN 99

SIXTEEN..107

SEVENTEEN 114

EIGHTEEN...120

NINETEEN 128

TWENTY 143

ONE

Lily 'Hart' Strom

> If I should die before you, cremate my body and commit my ashes to the ocean.
> —A note from Luke Strom to his sister

A month after my brother's remains were brought home in an earthenware urn, my father and I—my mother was still too distraught—took the container out to sea.

I remember that day well.

The sky was cloudy, the light tinged with pink. Windless. At the pier the driver of the chartered boat held out his hand, weathered to leather, to help us in. My father and I sat side by side on plastic cushions. I jammed my hands into the pockets of my wind jacket and my father lovingly cradled the urn. Neither of us spoke. The motor began and we sliced cleanly through the water, the cold salty morning air buffeting us, flattening our clothes against our bodies, and tearing at our hair.

When we were three nautical miles out, the driver cut the engine, and the boat began to gently drift. For a few seconds the air held only

the sounds of water lapping against the sides of the boat and the whispered creak of wood as my father and I moved toward the rail. The sea was a gray blank, quiet, waiting. Like a cemetery.

I stood beside him while he opened the mouth of the urn and undid the knot of the plastic bag inside. We each took a handful of the pale gray ash. One last touch.

'Oh, Luke,' I whispered brokenly, unable to reconcile that handful of *dust* with the living breathing being I had loved so dearly. When we were young we had been like Siamese twins, sharing one heart. Inseparable.

Without warning, it began to drizzle. I raised my eyes at the sky in surprise. Was it a sign? A final goodbye? Luke had always loved the rain. When he was young he used to cartwheel in it. Laughing, happy Luke. But the arms of my memories were cold. He was too young and sweet to die.

I began to cry.

Thousands of water droplets struck me and mingled with my silent tears as I stood perfectly still, fist stretched over the railing. I was aware of my father opening his hand, and the cloud of ashes pouring from it. As if that was not enough of a magic trick, he took the plastic bag out of the urn, and upended its contents into the sea. I watched Luke blossom in the water, temporarily disarmed by the gentle beauty of his new form. Finally I understood why they call incinerated bones white flowers in India.

My father turned to me.

I swallowed hard. I had no magic tricks up my sleeve. I had nothing.

Gently he nudged my arm. 'Let him go, Lily,' he urged, his voice lowered and solemn.

I looked up at him blankly. His blond eyelashes were wet with rain or tears or both, and in the milky light his eyes seemed paler than I had ever seen them. I noticed the deepening lines that fanned out from the corners of his eyes. Poor Dad. Somehow life had defeated him, too. I felt the first flash of helpless anger then.

With his left hand he wiped the damp strands of hair away from my cold cheeks. 'It will be OK,' he promised. He had no idea how hollow he sounded. His eyes flicked down meaningfully to my hand.

I nodded in agreement. Of course, it was what Luke wanted. And yet I could not open my fist. The drizzle became a freezing steady rain that plastered my hair to my head, and ran down my neck into my clothes, making me shiver. I could hear my father's voice in the background, like a distant buzz, pleading with me, but still I would not let my brother go. I could not. My hand was red and frozen tight.

Finally, my father pried his fingers into my tightly clenched fist and forced my hand open. Numb with horror, I watched the rain turn the ash into gray mud on my palm and wash Luke away forever.

On our way back the clouds opened to reveal a sky as brilliantly blue as my brother's eyes had been. So blue you could have wept.

I did.

TWO

I fell apart after that. No one could understand how painful it was for me. No one. They had *absolutely* no idea about the sharp teeth of guilt tearing at my insides, or the inescapable sorrow that wound itself around my heart like a thickly muscled anaconda tightening its hold every time I exhaled.

I had not been there for him.

My dreams became footsteps that kept taking me back to his killing ground. In my dreams I stood at his window, pale, limp, my hair waving like seaweed in water, and watched him push the needle into his arm. I was the witness. I was there to see the stair I had missed in the darkness.

I woke up in a trembling fury. Rage at everyone. No one was immune from it. Especially me. I sprang to the floor and like a caged animal paced my bedroom restlessly for hours at a time.

That last sniff of him—his perfume after the cells of his body had stopped replicating and replacing themselves—the bouquet of raw meat became a friend. Calling. Calling. Dangerously seductive. My existence had become hellish. I

wanted to escape. That day on the boat I had seen Luke become the ocean, the rain, the wind and the blue sky. I wanted all of that and Luke within me, too.

The otherworld… I nearly went.

After one failed attempt, while my mother looked at me with shocked, reproachful eyes, my despairing father who is a doctor quietly persuaded me to consider a temporary treatment of antidepressants.

'No one outside this family need ever know,' he said, the terrible guilt of not being able to save Luke skulking in his eyes.

I took the wretched things he gave me. They did the job. They banished my intolerable grief, but I lived in limbo, speaking only when spoken to, eating when food was put before me. And I think I might have been content to exist in that walking dream, on that cloud of dull edges forever, if not for the visit to the toxicologist.

It gave me a fresh pain. It woke me up.

Mr. Fyfield was small, assiduous, clean-cut, well groomed. He opened my brother's file as if that was the most important thing he had to do that day and in a funeral director's voice proceeded to explain some of the details contained within. I listened to his voice drift around the room idly until one sentence sent blood rushing up into my brain, so fast I felt it slam into my head.

Whoa! I opened my mouth and made an odd choking noise.

Both my parents turned to stare at me in surprise.

'But Luke died of an overdose,' I blurted out. My voice was unnatural, guttural.

Mr. Fyfield spared me an oddly sterile glance before returning his eyes to my parents. 'He overdosed because the heroin he consumed was spiked with acetyl fentanyl. Fentanyl is an opiate analgesic with no recognized medical use. It is typically prescribed to cancer patients as a last resort. It is five to fifteen times stronger than heroin and ten to one hundred times stronger than morphine.'

The jargon was difficult to comprehend in my state, but one fact was inescapable. I stared at Mr. Fyfield, wide-eyed and trembling. 'Knowing it could kill him...they sold it to him,' I whispered.

He looked at me as if I was either stupid or insanely naïve. 'I'm afraid so.'

I began to hyperventilate. My parents gathered around me protectively. I gasped that I needed a glass of water, which Mr. Fyfield's secretary immediately fetched. I drank it down and didn't say a word after that, but finally I was ready to start living again.

Over the next few days I decided that I would join the war on drugs. I made a promise to Luke's memory. I would do all I could to stop what had happened to him from happening to others. Anyone I saved would live because of Luke's memory.

I came off the pills. I did research. A lot of it. There were many agencies that I could have targeted, but I found myself gravitating toward undercover work. The idea of using deception to fight deception was perversely pleasing. But, more important, I thought it would be cool to no longer be Lily Strom, the basket case, but an alter ego. Someone new. I could decide who I wanted to be and build her from ground up.

There were two lines of work available as Test Purchase Officers (TPOs) and Undercover Officers (UCOs). Generally TPOs undertook a lower level of undercover work, usually presenting themselves as prostitutes or drug addicts to lure in the small-time dealers. Their assignments were unglamorous, quick in and out jobs that typically lasted only hours.

UCOs were a totally different kettle of fish. They lived in a different world, one shrouded in secrecy, taking on different names, different addresses and totally different ways of life, sometimes for years at a time. The most elite and secretive of these units was called SO10 or SCD10. So secret most police officers didn't even know it existed.

Although it was easier to be accepted as a TPO I knew I didn't want to be a TPO. My heart was set on being a UCO. They brought in the big fish. The kingpins. The ones I wanted to target.

'You'll have to finish your education if you want to be accepted in an agency like that,' my father said.

So I diverted all my rage and energy into work, graduated with honors, and applied to be a police officer. They accepted me and sent me to the Police Academy in Hendon. It was a flat, depressing place that looked exactly like one of those eyesore housing estates from the seventies; only it had a large swimming pool and a running track.

The training was undemanding: for twenty effortless weeks they taught us to unthinkingly and unquestioningly obey the chain of command at all times. But I was strangely glad of the strict parameters of authority that we had to conform to.

I came out of it a police officer.

THREE

One year later I stood in front of my commanding officer. 'I want to be in SO10,' I said.

He raised his eyes heavenward. 'They are a bunch of wannabe gangsters.'

That and all further arguments swayed me none at all. SO10 in my opinion was the pinnacle, the elite.

The very next day I made my way to New Scotland Yard carrying a docket of twenty-five pages of forms that I had painstakingly filled in and signed. I had made particular mention of the fact that I could speak Chinese, Norwegian, and my BA was in the Russian language.

On an upper floor, down a narrow, faceless corridor, I found a stable-style door with the magic words SO10 printed on a tiny sticker the size of a matchbox. Male voices and raucous laughter could be heard from within.

I took a deep breath—I had worked so hard and so long to get to this moment—and knocked on the top half of the door. There was no let-up to the mirth and voices within so I was startled when the top half of the door suddenly swung open.

Facing me was a bully of a man: close cropped red-brown hair, a navy blue North Face sweatshirt, gold sovereign rings on every finger, and an insufferably arrogant what-the-fuck-do-you-want expression on his face. It changed when he clocked me, though. In a totally leisurely and insulting way his gaze mentally undressed me. Eventually, his eyes traveled back to meet mine.

'The ladies' toilets are not on this floor, petal,' he advised, a patronizing smirk curling his lip.

'I…ah… I've brought my application form,' I stammered. I had never imagined such a blatantly sexist brush-off.

Reddish eyebrows flew upwards with exaggerated surprise. 'Yeah?'

I clutched my application form tightly and nodded.

'Give it to me, then,' he said. There could be only one way to describe his expression: highly amused.

He opened it and let his eyes run down it, sniggering and laughing intermittently. When he looked up his face was serious. 'Right then. You can go now.'

'Um… Someone will call me?'

'No doubt,' he said, in a tone that implied the opposite, and rudely closed the door in my face.

For a second I was too stunned to move and simply stood there. I heard him move into the room and say, 'You will *not* believe the skirt that just dropped this off.'

He must have then showed them my photo because the room broke out in low whistles and totally inappropriate comments. One guy said, 'Call a doctor, I think I've just caught yellow fever.' The group erupted in laughter. My face flamed.

Then a voice, more raspy and authoritative than all the others, said, 'Give that to me.' Later I would learn that his name was Mills—Detective Sergeant Mills.

Silence descended while he studied my form. I held my breath.

'Well, well,' Mills' voice pronounced mysteriously. 'Looks like we found the mouse to catch our lion.'

I turned away and ran down the stairs, my heart pounding like crazy. I knew then: I was going to be a UCO. But at that time I never thought about the logistics of the crazy idea of sending a mouse to catch a lion. I was just ecstatic: I *was* going to become an SO10 undercover officer.

Two days later I got a withheld number phone call from a woman administrator who said, 'You have been selected to join the SO10 team. Are you available to come in tomorrow?'

I gulped. Was I available? Bloody hell. 'Yes,' I replied smartly.

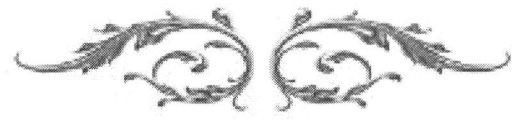

And just like that I was back at the stable door. This time, though, I had dressed conservatively in black tailored trousers, a white shirt that was buttoned close to the throat and a gray, loosely fitting jacket. My hair was pulled back in a tight ponytail and I wore no make-up. After the last visit I knew what I was in for. And I was not wrong.

The brute who had laughed at my application form came toward me. 'Get us some tea, will ya? Black, no sugar,' he said, as he passed me by.

I didn't miss a beat. 'Where's the kitchen?'

He pointed his thumb over his shoulder to indicate somewhere at the back.

I nodded. 'Anybody else want tea?'

There were two other guys there. Both had the same macho attitude.

'I'll have mine with milk and no sugar,' said one leaning back in his chair and stretching.

'Black. One sugar,' said the other without looking up from a book he was reading.

I nodded. No one was wearing name tags so I had no idea who anybody was and no one seemed inclined to introduce me.

I went into the kitchen, a small area with a microwave, toaster, a small fridge and a kettle. I found tea, sugar and milk, and from the back of a cupboard a tea-stained tray.

Just as I finished serving the men, another man walked in.

'Jolly good, tea. I'll have a cup, love. Two sugars and plenty of milk.'

I walked to the kitchen fuming, but my expression remained as cool as a cucumber.

I fixed the tea and put it in front of the man.

He waved vaguely toward some filing cabinets. 'How about putting some order into that fucking mess over there?'

'Right,' I said and walked toward it. He was right. It was a fucking mess. I decided to take all the files out and start from scratch.

'Come on,' a big, shaven-headed white man said as he walked past me. I recognized his voice. The man with the authority. I quickly jumped up and followed him into a small office.

'Close the door,' he said, as he lowered himself into his chair.

I obeyed. You could tell he had a hair-trigger temper just by looking at the tension in his shoulders. In fact, he reminded me of a standard issue brutish gangster.

'Sit.'

I sat.

'How's it going?'

'Great,' I said.

Something flicked very quickly across his eyes. 'Nice one. Off you go, then.'

Sorely disappointed, I stood up, thanked him and walked out of his office. I closed the door and another tough-looking guy walked in through the stable door.

'I'm gasping for some tea and toast,' he said, looking me right in the eye.

That morning I made twenty rounds of tea between bouts of 'administrative' work while they sat around regaling each other with tales of their bravery and the times when they had narrowly and heroically escaped death through relying purely on their wits. It became quickly obvious to me that the fastest way to gain their respect was to administer some sort of violence.

And the next day the routine was the same: round upon round of tea and toast and having to listen to their misogynistic and snide comments. But my grandmother had taught me, when you live in a lake you don't antagonize the crocodiles.

I was determined to stick it out and live in that infested lake. They were not going to break me. I was there for a reason and all those thinly veiled attempts to provoke me were not going to get a rise out of me. Although the atmosphere was macho, intimidating, and openly contemptuous of the rest of the police force, these men thought of themselves as the elite: I had not been brought there to make endless cups of tea. I knew I had something important they wanted. I was the mouse they needed to catch a lion. Let them have their fun until then.

On day five, Robin, one of the marginally nicer guys, stopped by my table where I was knee-deep in their antiquated filing system that still used paper receipts.

'Want to go out with us tomorrow?' he asked.

Going out with inarguably the most ignorant bunch of men I had ever had the misfortune to meet was not the most appealing offer I could think of, and there was also the distinct possibility that this was a means to humiliate me in public, but... 'Sure,' I said softly. 'Where are you guys going?'

'To a crack house.'

I smiled for the first time since I had come to SO10. 'Yeah, I do. I definitely do.'

'Great. Briefing is at eleven. You'll be going as a crack whore. So don't wash your hair and bring slutty clothes and skanky shoes with you.'

I nodded happily.

Finally!

FOUR

'Just relax. If it all goes pear-shaped a vanload of big guys in riot gear will rush in,' Robin said, while Federica, another undercover agent, expertly applied stage paint to make me look like a junkie.

I nodded, unable to stop staring at him. A very experienced ex TPO, he had incredibly transformed himself into a convincingly sad addict with a pasty face, bags under his eyes, greasy ropes for hair, fake ear and nose piercings, grimy nails, and stained clothes and shoes.

In a little hand-held mirror I watched Federica blacken my front teeth and paint a disgusting sore on one side of my mouth. When she was finished I stood still in a faux leather miniskirt, a purple Lycra tube top and cheap stilettos with heels that I had deliberately scuffed, while Jason fitted my 'technical' (body-worn recording equipment): an Apple iPod that had been equipped with a tiny camera and monitoring device that would allow the monitoring team to see and hear what was being said.

'Here,' Robin said, and gave me a battered packet of cigarettes. I unzipped my bag and put the packet into it.

'Rinse your mouth out with this,' Federica said holding out a bottle of red wine. I took it and swallowed a mouthful. Pure vinegar. Robin took it off me and glugged it down as if it was water.

'Ready?' he asked.

'Ready,' I said, shrugging into a filthy, fur-trimmed hooded parka. We got into a battered brown Renault and Jason drove us to the crack house. I sat in the back seat and mentally prepared myself for the unknown. I was going behind the locked doors of a real crack den to see the lost souls inside it.

It was two in the afternoon and the street was dead quiet. It was quite a nice area, actually. I wondered what the neighbors must think of having a crack den right in their midst.

Robin swiveled his head to look at me. 'Remember, the back door is welded shut, so don't ever make for it in an emergency.'

'I'll remember,' I said nervously.

He thumped a few times on the door and a black, well-built, twenty-something man with suspicious, darting eyes opened it. In his hand was a large hammer. This was not Robin's first time and the man—his name was Samson—touched fists with him and opened the door wider. I flashed Samson a quick smile, which was not returned, and totally ill at ease followed Robin and Federica into a darkened hallway.

 18

'When is he coming, bruv?' Robin asked.

'Soon, man,' Samson said with a Jamaican accent. 'Soon.'

Behind me I heard three heavy bolts slide shut.

For better or worse we were locked in with a man called Samson who was armed with a large hammer. Samson told Robin that the dealer had not arrived and that everybody was still waiting for him. He led the way to the living room, an *awful* room. There was neither furniture nor curtains. The windows were shrouded with moth-eaten blankets.

Crammed into that dim, smoky space were dozens of junkies leaning against the walls and sitting close together talking quietly. But from the flare when someone lit a cigarette or a crack pipe I saw the vacant desperation on all their faces. Humans of every race and age had been reduced to creatures that were beyond pitiful.

Their degradation and devastation was unbelievable. They were living corpses. Their stench couldn't be described. You had to experience it to believe the rotten reek of the accumulated weeping of the human body; blood, sweat, oil, urine; and dirt, layers upon layers of fetid filth.

It was *intolerable.*

There was also a great restlessness about them that made them appear to be a heaving mass united by a single all-consuming purpose. To score. They were all here for smack or crack.

Suddenly, fear gripped me that just as I could smell them, they could smell me. I felt wild-eyed with paranoia. Federica fitted her hand over mine and squeezed. I knew what it meant. *Calm down.*

I pressed her hand. *I hear you.*

Federica led me to a corner and we sat on the bare, dirty floor. I was glad to do so—my knees were shaking. I could not comprehend the utter wreck of the humanity around me. For a second I thought of Luke, the spoon on his coffee table, the rubber rope fallen on the floor, and the old tree of my sorrow shed a few leaves, but I pushed the thoughts away.

Not now, Lily Strom. Not now.

After a few minutes I came to realize that there was no talk of family or hobbies or work. Nothing. Just drugs. The only topic of conversation was about gear—they spoke about it endlessly. It was the only thing they lived for. And *everybody*'s main preoccupation was to know when the dealer would be arriving. Every once in a while someone would ask, 'When's he coming?' and the answer was always, 'Soon, man, soon.' I felt incredibly sorry for them, for their wasted lives. I thought of their parents and their sisters and maybe even their children.

Every few minutes more junkies knocked on the door. The place became more and more packed.

A gaunt man and his friend turned to me.

'Where you from, girl?' he asked.

It was only junkie small talk. Who were we? How did we hear about the house? The kind of thing that Robin had already briefed me I might be asked, but I was terrified I would slip up, or my accent would sound too forced and fake. So I started to pretend to be suffering from withdrawal systems, twitching, jerking, pulling faces and looking generally unwell, or I bit my nails furiously.

Federica fielded their questions expertly.

'Soon' turned out to be hours. I was exhausted from pretending to be in withdrawal. The longer I remained in that room the more anxious and worried I became. Finally, Samson announced that the dealer was five minutes away. The room became charged with an electric excitement; the mass began to prepare for its feast of delight.

Then a whisper spread like wildfire. 'He's here. He's here.' And everybody scrambled up from their sitting positions. Ready.

We heard the three bolts slide back, and the door opened.

The dealer, a strutting East Ender, in a Nike tracksuit, came with two minions. They immediately started dishing out the drugs to the addicts who had the presence of mind to line up as if they were in a supermarket queue. But some of them were so desperate by then that they lit up or stood against the walls shooting the drug into their veins instantly. Standing in the queue I gazed at one boy, high as a kite, bent from the waist swaying like a plant in the wind.

Robin, Federica and I produced our crumpled tenners and got our little rocks of crack.

When it was my turn the minion looked directly into my eyes and my throat constricted. An Eastern European *boy*. He couldn't have been more than nineteen. I held out my two tenners.

'One of each, please.'

I noticed the notes were trembling, but he snatched them from me, and gave me a tiny white rock (crack) wrapped in white plastic and a small brown rock (heroin) in blue plastic. I closed my fingers around them and... Suddenly all hell broke loose.

The riot boys were coming in. The door imploded with an enormous crash at the same time as the windows were being smashed to smithereens. To the sound of splintering glass they were pouring in screaming, 'Police, police,' ordering everyone to, 'Show your hand.'

It was like being caught in a tornado. I had never seen anything like it before. Helmeted, flameproof balaclavas and massive in their heavy-duty uniform, some were wearing glass suits (special material that protected them when they climbed windows full of glass splinters). They mowed into the gaunt addicts, screaming, 'Get on the fucking floor. Now.' And beating them with batons. The poor junkies! *The war on drugs was total crap! A political sleight of hand.*

Both the drug dealer and I had frozen in terror. He looked at me—his eyes were wide with fear. In that second I realized that he was no tough kingpin, but a frightened little boy who was as much a victim as the desperados he served. The small-time drug dealers were just as vulnerable and in need of *real* help as the addicts were. He, me, Luke we were all victims. At that moment: did he know? Who I was?

Then he was running to flush the drugs. He didn't know Federica had already blocked the toilet. He ran straight into a beefy figure in black. One second after he was pushed face first into a wall. I was toppled. A large officer pressed my face into the ground and I felt the grit and the dirt from the filthy floor scrape into my skin. The two rocks in my hand fell out.

The cuffs were on me in seconds. 'You're nicked. Possession of Class A drugs,' the officer gleefully proclaimed.

'Just do exactly as you are told,' Federica muttered under her breath next to me.

I went limp.

Then, just as suddenly as it had begun, it was all under control. They had completely trashed the place and everybody was in cuffs. Incredibly, it had all lasted only seconds.

I could see Robin play-acting, calling the cops 'cunts', and Federica was yelling abuse in Italian, but I could also see that they were high on the adrenalin of a successful bust-up. Of knowing they had closed down another despicable crack house. I knew I should have felt the same, but I was too much in shock. I could not forget the look in the drug dealer's eyes. None of those

23

arrested would be given the help that they desperately needed, and were too ill to obtain themselves. They would simply be holed up somewhere for some time and then released, and the whole cycle would repeat again. This was a war where there would be no winners, only 'good' crime figures, praise from superiors, and more funding for the drug squad.

Out through the smashed door I staggered in the bright light of the afternoon. I could have wept from the relief of the light. I took deep gulps of fresh air and turned my face upwards as if in prayer. For a few seconds my soul blossomed and then I was roughly uprooted as if I was no more than a dandelion that does not belong and pushed into a waiting drug squad car. I looked out of the window and saw that neighbors had gathered to watch. One of them met my eyes. There was no pity or compassion, only condemnation and disgust in her face. I was just another junkie fouling up her neighborhood.

I turned to the arresting officer. 'I'm a cop. I'm a UCO.' It ran hollow. So hollow it echoed in my brain.

And so hollow the cop said sarcastically, 'No doubt.'

I said nothing else until Robin came to get me at the local police station where we had been taken.

'We got them,' he said, still buzzing.

'And you were great,' Federica added. She looked elated.

I was too shocked and shaken to reply. I felt my lip start trembling and tears welling up behind my eyes, but somehow, I clenched my teeth, swallowed my emotions and put on a brave face. I realized that both of them had known that it was not going to be a simple test purchase exercise. It was a full-blown bust-up, but they had not informed me because it had been a test of sorts.

I was not going to fail by falling apart.

I wanted their report to note that I was strong.

That I was the mouse to catch a lion.

FIVE

The next morning I stood in DS Dickie Mills' spartan office. He used to be a UCO—for many years. Now he was top brass running the Met's covert ops program together with five other undercover officers. He drove a 7 Series BMW and was unashamedly and brazenly tough as nails.

He was wearing a gray Armani polo neck, cream trousers with knife edge creases, and Prada loafers. When he rested his palms on the edge of his desk his gold Rolex peeked through.

'There's an undercover course in two days' time. I want you on it.'

'Yes, sir.'

'Get the details from Robin.'

'Yes, sir,' I responded confidently.

'That will be all.'

'Thank you, sir.'

'Come and see me after... If you pass.'

The undercover course, held at Hendon Training Centre, turned out to be a two-week long, bloody hard training session packed with interrogations, role-plays, cameos, pretend UC operations in real time, psychometric tests, psychological evaluations, and a final interview with cold-eyed UC officers.

There were twelve of us on the course. If I had thought my Police Academy training was a means of sucking the recruits' individuality out and brainwashing them to unquestioningly obey the chain of authority at all times, then the undercover course was breaking down and hardwiring recruits on steroids.

For two weeks we were kept tired, stressed and disorientated with an incredibly intensive schedule and lack of sleep. Once I went to bed at 5.30 a.m. and had to be back in the classroom at 8.00 a.m. Our tutors frequently subjected us to abuse and degrading names. One even called me a cunt. Three students were simply arbitrarily dismissed and we never saw them again. Two broke down in tears and left.

We were expected, in fact compelled, to drink until the early morning hours with the staff and

sometimes with the role-play carried on throughout the night to see if we could keep our created personas when we were drunk. Even the weekends brought no respite—we were given tasks that necessitated us traveling all over London and finishing at midnight.

My first time in the interrogation chair left me a shaking mess. I was supposed to take on the persona of a runaway turned stripper who dabbled in drugs and was looking for a job in a lap dancing joint. Tensely, I took the chair and perched on the end of it nervously. They began.

First they lulled you into a sense of false confidence by asking simple questions. With me it was the kind of drugs I had taken.

Easy. I felt myself relax.

Then they asked me for the street prices of those drugs.

I sailed through those.

Then they asked about the last hostel I had stayed in.

I was prepared. I told them.

'What street is it on?'

I swallowed. I knew that. I had memorized it. But my mind was a blank.

'Is it the one near Aldi supermarket?' one of them asked, his eyes gleaming, sensing weakness.

I floundered. I had absolutely no idea. 'I'm not sure. I didn't go out much,' I evaded. Black thoughts swirled in my head. After all this, I was not going to pass, after all. I felt so bad the tears

pricked at the backs of my eyes, but crying, I knew, would only make them jeer and hound me mercilessly. I had seen them heap abuse on others for crying. I bit my lip hard and looked them in the eye.

'So who was running the hostel that year, then?'

Oh shit. 'I... I've forgotten,' I stammered.

'This is fucking bullshit,' he roared.

'Load of old bollocks,' the other interrogator agreed, fixing me with a mean stare.

I was falling apart inside, but I kept my face calm. 'Look, I didn't want to say this before, but when I was in that hostel I was a total wreck. I took so many drugs I didn't know whether I was coming or going,' I said in a contrite tone of someone confessing.

I batted more questions. By the time I rejoined the others I was shaking with nerves and exhilaration. The fuckers had not broken me down.

By the end of the course, I was mentally exhausted, and had lost nearly half a stone in weight. There were five of us left standing. There were no awards or medals or ceremony to tell us we had passed. We just gathered in a restaurant for a meal and that was that.

Two of us went off to join foreign forces, another two were taken as part of the part-time index, which meant that they would be available for part-time UC work alongside their day job in whatever police department they belonged to.

And I alone was taken on as part of the full UC unit.

I had passed!

SIX

DS Mills swiveled his large black chair and contemplated the bleak gray sky outside his window, as I stared in wonder at the chiseled, savagely handsome face of Jake Eden—a.k.a. Crystal Jake, the kingpin drug dealer. I could hardly believe it. The assignment was for me to infiltrate one of the Eden family clubs and find out how their secretive and vast drug empire was run.

Ever since I joined the police force all I had ever dreamed of had been just such an opportunity. Going after the big guys. Making a difference. To think that such a plum assignment had fallen so easily into my hands was shocking. I wanted to punch the air.

I put the photograph carefully back into the thin file it had come out of and picked up the photos of his brothers: Shane and Dominic Eden. Both extremely good-looking, but without that dangerous panther-ish quality of their brother.

'We've been wanting to insert an agent into his organization for some time, but it needed to be the right person.'

I looked up at DS Mills. He was watching me expressionlessly. 'What makes me right?'

'The man at the helm of this evil gang is so mysterious and secretive that he is almost mythical. He trusts no one. Using a male officer in these circumstances would likely yield no result and could be dangerous for the operative. Gypsies have their own ways of dealing with snitches.'

'And I'm the spider who will lure him into our web?'

'Something like that,' he admitted impatiently, obviously disgruntled by the analogy I had used. 'We're hoping that by inserting you into one of his clubs you will eventually meet him or one of his brothers and over time you will attempt to disarm one of them with your abundance of charm. These tinker families are close-knit. There are no secrets between them. One is as good as the other to bring Crystal Jake to his knees.'

I frowned. There was a touch of bitterness and envy in DS Mills' voice. I wondered if this was a personal vendetta.

'This is a level one assignment. High risk and long term. It requires someone intelligent with social insight, able to react quickly and adapt accordingly to situations. You will be living under your assumed identity for months and socializing with people that you must never forget are the enemy that you have been employed to finger. These are cunning, ruthless criminals who will kill to protect what is theirs.' Mills kept his small, sharp eyes trained on me:

seeking out my fears or telltale signs of weakness. If I was going to back out, this was my opportunity to walk away.

But I kept my expression as impassive and calm as the surface of a lake. He could *never* know what a seething mess lurked deep beneath. 'This is what I trained for, sir.' I noticed my voice was shaking.

Mills' eyes searched me relentlessly for what seemed like minutes, but was obviously only moments. He frowned suddenly. A look of uneasiness crossed his features. Had he seen under the surface of the lake? But if he had, he had decided to ignore it. People were expendable to DS Mills. What was important was a job well done. And more commendations for him. 'Good,' he said curtly. 'But be warned—do not underestimate Eden, he is a formidable man, a persuasive man with the ladies. And do not *ever* trust him no matter how close you get. Your life may depend on it...'

The sharpness of DS Mills' tone was resoundingly clear. Suddenly, an unfamiliar feeling stirred the tiny hairs on my arms, and I didn't know whether to feel terrified or excited about meeting Jake Eden. But I was certain that when I did my heart would be like a rock— strong, unflinching.

'Robin will sort your cover alter ego with you.' A semblance of a smile escaped. The interview was nearly over.

'Sir, can I just ask, why me?'

 33

His eyes shifted downwards. He hesitated, but he knew it was a valid question.

He smiled. It was rather unpleasant. 'I guess it comes down to your looks.'

'My looks, sir?' My face was flaming. So it had nothing to do with my language skills or the accomplishments in my CV then.

Mills showed me a concealed skill, an adeptness in diplomacy that had once propelled him to become one of Britain's best UC officers. 'A hardboiled, experienced officer would be no good. You have the right amount of innocence and mystery. I believe you could be Crystal Jake's Achilles heel.'

My eyebrows rose in shock. This was not what I had signed up for. 'You want me to sleep with him?'

'On the contrary. That would be improper and illegal. Such an activity could only be as an abject failure of the deployment and a gross abuse of your role and position as an officer of the Met. If he sleeps with you, you are finished. He will discard you like an old shirt. I want you to flirt with him. Tease him. Court him. In the old-fashioned way.'

I nodded, but I was confused. It seemed an impossible task. First that such a man would be interested in me and second that I would be able to keep him on such a tenuous string. It was more likely that sexual relationships between covert deployed officers and those they were employed to infiltrate and target were not officially sanctioned or authorized, but I could read between the lines. What he was really telling me was that Crystal Jake would lose interest in me as soon as he had had me! And that was why I was not to sleep with him.

'If you cannot get to Crystal, then suck up to one of the brothers. You sure you're up to this task, Strom? It's not going to be a quick or an easy one and you're going to have to keep your wits about you.'

'Never been more sure of anything, sir,' I replied firmly.

'By the way...' His eyes flicked to my nails, bitten to the quick. 'You'll need a new set of nails.'

'Yes, sir.'

When I came out of Mills' office I saw that the other officers were gathered around Mark's desk. Mark was the man who had taken my form that first day.

'A piss,' he was saying, as he put his feet up on his desk.

Ah well, more testosterone-fueled posturing, telling stories of jobs gone by and bragging about who had brought in the biggest cache of guns or drugs: the usual dick swinging contest. I noticed that Robin was not around.

'Who wants some tea and biscuits?' I called out.

'Sure. Get us a round,' someone shouted. The rest of them laughed. The mood was jolly, as it usually was around there.

I smiled brightly. I went into the kitchen and made them all tea, just the way they liked it. I brought it out and handed them their mugs.

'One sugar, two sugars, milk, black.'

Then I went to my table and noticed that since I had been gone the filing system had gone to pot again. I was gathering all the files that had not yet been properly categorized into a pile in the middle of my desk when I heard the first howl of fury. I looked up calmly. Mark was looking at me with a murderous expression. He had spewed the coffee all over his desk and some had spilled onto his precious Ralph Lauren trousers. Two others looked like they had had a sip of their tea, too. The others were warily putting their mugs down.

I dumped all the files back into the cupboard and smiled at them. Surprised. For a group of people that were always taking the piss out of others they had turned out to be pretty thin-skinned.

I had used salt instead of sugar.

SEVEN

Robin grinned at me. 'If you want to bag a tiger you need the right equipment. You need a whole new set of clothes, bank account, the works. We need to create a package your targets cannot resist.'

'Ready when you are,' I replied, with a fierce thrill of excitement.

'First, we'll have to install you in a rented flat.'

And that was how I came to be sharing a flat in South London with another UC officer, but she was never there as she had her own 'other' life. Then for four months Robin and I painstakingly constructed my alibi and cover story.

'We usually use our real Christian names,' he said. 'If someone from your old school recognizes you from across the street the hope is that they will simply call out your Christian name.'

I nodded, but I had pushed all my friends away after Luke died.

'Do you have a name you'd like to assume?'

'Hart,' I said immediately. 'Lily Hart.'

'Right, time to apply for a passport dating from three years back and a driving license.'

'Why would a runaway have a passport?'

'Because she toyed with the idea of dancing in Amsterdam?'

They arrived in less than a week. Both fake passport and DVLA issued driving license had been created in collusion with the appropriate governmental departments and were good for travel and if I was stopped by the police. Using those, I opened bank accounts and applied for credit cards.

Robin took me to lap dancing clubs so I could watch the girls, the way they behaved, and how they interacted with their customers. I saw them rub their naked flesh against men and I thought I had cringed inwardly, but Robin must have sensed my discomfort.

'The most important thing I learned, first and foremost,' he said quietly, 'was that whatever I was doing, I had to always remember that I was a police officer.'

I turned to him. His face was unusually serious.

'Don't allow yourself to get psychologically mixed up. Always keep what you are doing and who you are separate. At the end of the operation you will ditch all the physical trappings of your undercover alter ego, the hair, the clothes, the people you have befriended, and return to your own normal world.'

'Is that really possible?' I asked, surprised.

He looked me in the eye. 'You have to. If you don't maintain the line between the job and who you really are you will become a wreck. For

example, if you find yourself in a position where you have to take a drug then you have to come out of that personality as soon as possible and tell your handler, in your case DS Mills. And if necessary you will have to go for counseling.'

'Will I have to take drugs?' I asked worriedly.

'No, we will put it into your cover story that you've had a very bad experience, nearly died, et cetera, and no longer touch the stuff.'

'When and how do I start asking for information?'

'Work your way in very slowly,' Robin said. 'This is a long-term assignment and so requires a huge element of deception. We don't want the target to get suspicious. He is very intelligent, wary, and uncommonly aloof. Don't appear too eager for information. In fact, don't ask for any information. Let some chances to ask for information go by. Don't even appear curious. Lull him into a place of complete trust before you sink the hooks in.'

He then warned me that constant fear of discovery and letting the side down, which was part and parcel of undercover work, could manifest itself as sexual arousal. 'Watch for it and be prepared for it.'

That night he also introduced me to Anna.

Over the next two months she gave me pole-dancing lessons and taught me some really cool moves that looked good and professional, but didn't take an athlete to perform.

A week before I was due to start my assignment I had my nails done and glamorous red highlights put into my hair. I looked into the mirror. There. My alter ego was ready to be unleashed.

On the day before I was due to meet Patrick, who would take me on my audition at Eden, I went to see my parents. We had dinner together at a restaurant. The hole that was Luke was bigger than ever. My father told me he was very proud of me.

'When will you come to see us?' my mother said, crying quietly.

'I don't know, but I will call.' The reality was I wanted my new life to begin. I wanted to stop being Lily Strom and begin my new existence as Lily Hart.

I had become quite close to Robin and on that morning before I left to start my assignment he hugged me. His parting words were, 'Never let your guard down. Remember, one false move can give you away.'

But what stayed in my mind and haunted me was what he had once told me when we were dining at a Chinese restaurant. He told me the loneliest place in the world was the place inhabited by the undercover police officer when they are deep inside the mind of a fictional person.

Take me down to the paradise city
Where the grass is green
And the girls are pretty
Take me home
(Oh won't you please take me home?)
—Guns 'N' Roses, *Paradise City*

BOOK 2

EIGHT

Lily Hart

Have you ever been compelled to take a step that you know is a mistake but you simply can't stop?

The return home from the Tate Modern is a blur. I walk through the streets of London blindly, telling myself over and over again that I did it for Luke. I try to remember him, but his image eludes me. All I see is Jake, shirtless on a horse, Jake looking at me. Jake standing blood-splattered in Melanie's apartment. Jake with tears in his eyes. Jake holding me. Jake kissing me. Jake smiling. Jake laughing. Jake. Jake. Jake.

I stop walking and hold my head. It feels as if it is about to burst.

'Are you all right?' someone asks.

I look up. A man is looking at me. He seems concerned. 'Yes,' I say automatically. Nothing could be further from the truth.

'OK,' he says, and moves on.

Robin's words flash into my mind.

At the end of the operation you will ditch all the physical trappings of your undercover alter ego, the hair, the clothes, the people you have befriended, and return to your own normal world.

A small, hesitant voice in my head asks, what about the people you fall in love with? I drum it out with the militant message they have brainwashed me with. *First and foremost you are a police officer.*

I *have* done the right thing.

I walk until my legs start to ache, then I stop and hail the first taxi I see. Inside it, I sit with my face turned toward the window, seeing nothing. The taxi drops me outside the house. I watch it drive away and stand at the bottom of the short flight of steps for an age. My legs are like lead. Eventually, my heart weeping, I climb the steps.

I open the front door and I know straight away: he is home. I walk down the corridor and open the living room door.

Seeing him is like jumping into an icy river. The guilt. God, the guilt. I know: I'm in too deep. I have broken the most important rule—I didn't keep what I am doing and who I am separate. I have allowed myself to get psychologically mixed up.

He is sitting on the white leather sofa, but he must have been pacing the floor until he heard me at the front door, because there is that look of restlessness about him. A glass of Scotch sits on the table. He looks pale under his tan and his green eyes burn feverishly bright in his face.

I smile as I shatter inside. The heaviest tears never reach the eyes.

 44

He doesn't smile back. He seems very still. His eyes hold onto me so hard it almost hurts.

'Hi,' I say.

'Where have you been?' I see that his hands are clenched hard and he seems to be controlling himself.

'I was shopping.'

His chest heaves and his eyes flick to the bag in my hand. 'Why did you not answer your phone?'

'I had it on silent.'

He nods gently, but seems somehow inconsolable. I feel the vibrations of his despondency in my blood as if it were my own.

'I'm sorry, I didn't think you would worry,' I murmur.

He takes a deep breath. Again I see him making a Herculean effort to control himself. 'You were attacked less than a week ago, Lily.'

'I'm really sorry,' I say again.

'You look tired,' he observes.

'I am.' I try to smile at him.

'Come here.'

I go to him and climb into his lap. His hands come around me, the palms hot. I nuzzle him like a cat, my hand stroking his thick hair, straightening it. It is ruffled. He has been running his hands through it. He takes my shoes off and lets them drop with a thud on the floor. I sigh with pleasure when his big hands start massaging my foot.

'I didn't know where you were. If you had simply run away. I know so little about you.' His voice is a deep, honeyed rumble. It has a song in it. I could listen to it all my life. But I won't. I was fooling myself before.

'I didn't run away. I'm here.'

The hardness between his legs pushes into my hip. I look up into his eyes. There is only one word for what is in them: *hunger*. I have never seen such extreme desire, such ravenous craving. The air trembles with it. A voice inside my head cries, 'What have you done? What have you done?' I ignore it. My body loses its tiredness and responds to that yearning. My lips part, my nipples swell and pebble tightly, my sex opens like a night flower.

'Would it be really horrible if we had sex right now?' he murmurs.

'Yes, that would be utterly, utterly horrible.'

He carries me to the bedroom and kicks the door open. The large chandelier is not lit. Instead only the narrow bronze lamps over the paintings on the walls are on, creating their own individual pools of yellow light, making the paint look thick and oily. I glance at the bed and my mouth opens with astonishment. I turn back to look at his face. 'What the—?'

'Indulge me,' he says languidly and throws me on the bed covered thickly with money.

'Oh,' I gasp.

'Get naked,' he orders.

Giggling, I pull my top over my head and, lifting the upper half of my body slightly, unclasp my bra and pull it off. I raise my hips off the bed and shimmy out of my skirt. There are only my panties left.

'Help me,' I say.

He reaches down and, sliding his hands along my bare thighs, pulls them down my legs and flings them over his shoulders.

Hungrily he looks down at me lying naked on a bed of money. I gaze up at him, and slowly biting my lower lip, grab two handfuls of money, and throw them up into the air. They fall over and around me.

'Hello,' I say, covered in his dirty money.

He nods slowly, formally. As if he approves of my actions. We continue to stare at each other. I could have stayed there looking up at him forever. I actually feel faint with longing. He is so beautiful, I want to reach out and touch his skin to see if he is real.

'Do it again.'

I lift handfuls of money and pour them onto my body. One note lands on my mouth. I blow it away. Here I am, an undercover cop, bathed in money, about to fuck a criminal, and not wanting to be anywhere else in the world.

He gets down on his haunches and cupping my buttocks in his large hands, lifts my hips bodily and, bringing my open sex toward his face, deeply sniffs in my female scent. I have been walking all day and I imagine the smell to

be scandalously strong and musky. But I am not embarrassed. I know he likes dirty sex. This is the man who thinks warm raw sea urchin tastes good.

He lets his tongue swirl between the pink folds. The velvet brush is succulent, bringing with it whispers of sensations. Deep within I begin to tremble indescribably. My body instinctively arches, and my hips grind into his mouth, feeling his teeth, and begging for more and more. He slips his fingers into me. I grab his head and force it against me. With his fingers impaled inside me, his tongue works my clit.

'Get up on your elbows and let me look at you.'

I obey his demand and look into his eyes. They look stunning. He gazes into my glazed ones. Suddenly, I can't hold his gaze. I am the dirt that has betrayed him. I close my eyes.

'Open your eyes and look at what I am doing to you.'

I open my eyes and, unable to meet his eyes, watch his mouth fasten down on my sex and suck it like a hungry babe at its mother's breast. My body feels no guilt. It pushes me on until I break apart with a stifled cry inside his mouth, his fingers deep inside, his eyes trained on me, my head thrown so far back it touches the wings of my shoulder blades.

I lift my head slowly.

He is watching me, his lips shining with my juices. 'I like watching you lose control.'

I flop back down on the bed, roll over, and getting on my hands and knees, money sticking to my damp skin, offer my throbbing, eager sex up to him.

'Lay your face on the bed,' he growls. The sound wells up from deep inside him.

I hear the sound of his trousers hitting the floor as I lie on my cheek. The scent of money rises into my nostrils: soiled ink, slightly disagreeable. He grabs my hips, and, with a snarl of hungry desire, plunges into me. His cock feels more swollen than usual, voluptuous. I marvel at the sensation even as my muscles ripple around him to accommodate the intrusion. Coated in hot, slick juices he pushes in harder. I tilt my hips so he slides in deeper.

'Who does this hole between your legs belong to, Lily?'

'You,' I gasp, as another thrust makes more notes detach from my body and rain down on the bed.

Another thrust. 'Say it again.'

'You,' I pant.

'And who do you belong to?'

'You. I belong to you.'

And with that he explodes inside me, wild, hot cum shooting into me.

I hear him breathing hard. With me still speared to his body, he leans forward, his body barely brushing my back. He kisses me on the base of my neck where there is a little nerve that makes me shiver, and whispers in my ear, his

breath hot and moist, 'You can keep all the money you can hold in your hands.'

Baffled, my spine prickling, I turn my head back to look at him. Is he…?

But his face is innocent.

He moves back and pulls out of me. My body immediately misses him. I watch his eyes latch onto the blood-engorged, reddened flesh between my legs, his milky seed seeping out.

I can read his mind. If I stay in that position one moment longer he will slide his fingers into me. I crawl forward and sit cross-legged on the money. There is a note stuck to my calf. I peel it off, thinking of Melanie, thinking of her saying, 'I take their money and spend it and that is my revenge.'

Dust motes are swirling magical specks in the last rays of the evening's sun pouring in through the windows.

I let my gaze travel over the notes. They are mostly tens and twenties. There must be at least fifty thousand pounds I am sitting on. I could ask where the money has come from, but I remember Robin saying, *Let some chances to ask for information go by. Don't even appear curious. Lull him into a place of complete trust before you sink the hooks in.* So he wants to play the games low-level gangsters employ to show off to their women? When again our eyes clash my face is calm, my thoughts hidden.

'Do I have a time limit?' I ask.

'Nope.'

'OK.' I start gathering the money, carefully, in bricks. Afterwards, without looking at him, but knowing he is watching me, I slide the bricks together. Six bricks. I double them so their height will be slightly higher than my palm and fingers spread to their fullest. I push them together and notice a note lying on the floor. I look up at Jake, standing with his arms crossed over his chest.

I arch an eyebrow. 'Do you mind?'

Wordlessly he bends, picks it up, and holds it out to me. I take it and, putting it on top of my pile of bricks, lift them all by pressing them together on either side of the tower with my spread palms. The whole thing comes up in between my palms.

I look up at him, fifty thousand pounds richer.

He grabs my hand—the bricks fall down on the bed in a heap—and pulls my naked body to his. 'Do you know what I am thinking?' he mutters.

My heart somersaults. I take his lower lip between my teeth and pull it experimentally as far away from his face as I can while my hands start undoing the top button of his shirt. He drags his lips in a trail of fire along my throat and my chin and catches my mouth with his. His tongue delves in, seeking mine, like a grounded child whose friend has come to knock on the door to ask if he can come out to play.

'Someone should bottle you,' he says softly, much, much later.

NINE

Jake

The sound of a bird chirping wakes me up. Shit. That's no fucking bird in my bedroom. Immediately I tense. It can only be bad news. I feel Lily moving in the pitch dark. Her bedside lamp comes on. She blinks and squints blearily against the glare of the light. I lay a hand on her shoulder.

'Go back to sleep,' I say softly, and quickly go out of the room holding my phone. The light clock flashes 3.50 a.m.!

'What is it, Dom?' My voice is not sleepy. It is a bark, at once urgent, worried and irritated. I run down the stairs.

'They've only gone and torched Eden, haven't they?' He sounds like he has been drinking.

My stomach lurches. My first thought: 'Where's Shane?'

'He's all right,' my brother says instantly.

I feel almost sick with relief.

Without drawing breath Dom carries on ranting, 'It was the Pilkingtons that did it. I

52

fucking know it was that big bastard. No one else would dare.'

I get into the living room and start walking toward the window. 'Calm down, Dom.'

'Calm down? Calm down?' he bellows. 'I'm gonna kill him. I'll fucking kill the ugly vermin. These motherfuckers need to know who they're messin' with. I say I get some of our boys to Red Ice and turn it into a nice bonfire tomorrow night.'

This is not good. Dom is in one of his volcanic rages. I can picture him, his lean, wiry body crashing about whatever room he is in, his neck popping with purple veins, his mind an unthinking red mist. I need to calm him down. The situation is bad enough without another bonfire. Outside it is beautifully still.

'Take it easy, Dom.'

'Are you kidding me? That lowlife scum is trying to muscle in on our patch and you're asking me to take it easy? He'll be dead meat before I call this feud between the Edens and the Pilkingtons over,' he screams into my ear.

'Shut up. Your head is fucked,' I snarl furiously.

That gets through to him. He goes silent.

I take a deep breath. 'Let me think. We need to remain calm and focused,' I say seriously.

'And then what?' he spits, still boiling, but disaster has been averted for now.

My temples begin to throb. This silly generational feud. Will I never be free of it? Still, I'm in no mood to argue.

'And then *I* decide. I'm the head of this family and don't you forget it.'

Dom subsides like a soufflé that has seen daylight too early. 'OK, I hear you. I'm sorry. What do you want me to do, Jake?'

'Take your boys and go down there and see what the gossip is and report back to me in the morning.'

'All right, I'm gonna do what you ask, but this needs to be sorted quickly. I'm not gonna let that cocky cunt walk all over us—'

I terminate the call and fling my mobile across to the couch. Shit, fucking shit. The last thing I need is for Dominic to go crashing into this delicate truce between the Pilkingtons and the Edens. Nobody can even remember anymore why our two families are feuding, but we are. We stay out of each other's way. Why on earth would the Pilkingtons decide to reignite the feud now? There is no sense to it. Neither of us wants an all-out war. I call Shane.

He answers on the first ring. 'Dom called you?' He sounds stressed.

'Yeah. Where are you now?'

'At the club.'

'Is the fire out?'

'Yeah, looks like it.'

'How bad is it?'

'They firebombed the front and the back. There was hardly anything to burn in the front and the sprinklers contained the fire but the kitchen looks bad.'

'Do you need me to come there?'

'Nah. I got it under control. The police are here now.'

'Right. I'll see you in the morning.'

I flick on a light switch, go to the bar, and reach for a bottle of Scotch. I pick it up to down it and see Lily is standing at the door. I take a swallow, my fingers gripping the cold glass.

'You want a drink, Lil?'

Before she can answer I pour a second shot into another tumbler. I walk up to her, pass her the drink and raise my glass against hers. I swallow in one but she doesn't even pretend to drink.

'What's going on, Jake?'

'Someone set fire to Eden.'

'What?' Her eyes widen with shock. 'Why?'

I shrug. 'Could be just kids.'

'Do you have to go there now?'

'No, Shane is there.'

'Do you need me to do anything?'

I shake my head and kiss her on the top of her head. 'Go back to bed. I've got some calls to make. I'll be in shortly.'

'OK.' She turns around and starts walking toward the bedroom.

'Oh, Lil, would you like to go on a trip tomorrow?'

She turns around slowly. 'By myself?'

'Of course not. With me, obviously.'

She beams at me. 'Of course I would.'

I feel that dizzy rush to my head. It is unbelievable how crazy I am about her. She is waiting for me to explain. Tell her where or why. But I don't and she walks away from me. Smiling, but confused.

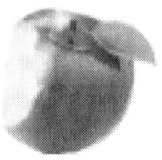

Lily

I don't close the door to the living room and go back to bed. Instead I stand at the top of the stairs and listen, but there are no more sounds to be heard other than Jake going into the dining room and shutting the door behind him. I go back to the bedroom and lie on the bed.

So the Pilkingtons have firebombed Eden. I frown. The information in the file Mills gave me clearly stated that both crime families maintain distant but cordial relations, and have their areas clearly drawn up. If it was the Pilkingtons, there is no doubt that this is a declaration of war. But why? There is no benefit to either family to engage in all-out turf war.

Hours later, when a small sliver of light seeps under the curtain, Jake comes back to bed. I pretend to be asleep. He stands over me watching me sleep. I keep my breathing even and deep. Eventually, he goes over to his side of the bed. I can hear him peeling off his clothes before the mattress gives way to his weight.

I make a small sound, as if I have just woken up, and turning around mumble incoherently. He is sitting with his back to me, but his head is turned down to look at me. I blink up at him. In the blue light of dawn his back is an intriguing play of shadows and gleaming muscles, but his eyes are densely black.

All I want to do is grab his silky hair and drag his mouth onto mine. This is exactly the moment of vulnerability that I have been waiting for. It must be exploited. I reach out a hand, and a frisson of electricity goes through me when our skins touch.

'It's not just random kids, is it?'

'Probably not,' he admits very softly.

'You know who it is, don't you?'

His voice is guarded. 'Maybe.'

'Why did they do it?'

He sighs. 'I don't know yet, but I intend to find out.'

'Why are we going away tomorrow?'

'Because I need to think.'

'Where are we going?'

'Ibiza.'

 57

I could have pushed more, but suddenly I am filled with an odd and surprising sensation. Not to take or break. But the acute regret that I am unable to savor him, as I would a fine wine. If only I was his real girlfriend. If only he could really trust me. If only I could help him instead of finding a way to trap him.

The thoughts are burdensome. Willfully breaking what I have believed in for so long. But mostly because they betray the promises I have made to Luke. And I am faithful if nothing else. My loyalty must be to Luke at all times.

He lies down beside me. For a while there is only the sound of our breathing.

'I'm here for you,' I whisper. And the odd thing is I mean it.

He turns his head to look at me. Our gazes meet and hold. The look in his eyes is so intoxicating I can't look away.

'Thank you,' he says, and his voice is strangely breathless.

TEN

Lily

Jake's house in Ibiza is a triumph of cubist modernist architecture. Set into the clifftop it is held up by an impressive framework of poured concrete, steel columns and beams. A concealed garage opens remotely.

'Wow,' I exclaim.

'That's what I said when I saw the artist impression of the design.'

At the entrance, a suspended steel framed cube hovers in mid-air while the frameless pivot door welcomes us into a stunningly minimalist entrance hall. It opens out to a space into which natural light pours through floating roofs. Sliding doors and the extensive use of glass make the threshold between the open plan interior and exterior convincingly invisible.

Jake slides open the glass doors and we are standing outside facing a swimming pool. Beyond it is the blue-green sea. It is so beautiful my breath catches. Now I know why he wanted to come here to think. This place is so modern and yet so wild and natural. It's taken me some time but I am slowly starting to understand him a little better. He is a sensuous man who needs wildness, nature. They are almost a part of him. That is why he rides horses bareback.

For a while we are both silent, drinking in the salty sea breeze. Then he looks down at me, tousled, but somehow refreshed already.

'Come, I'll show you the rest of the house.'

Natural light floods even the deepest parts of the house and there is always that sense of space that comes from vast expanses of glass. There are two receptions, three bedrooms all facing the sea, a kitchen, a dining room, and a cellar. We don't go down into it.

He opens the freezer and takes out a bag. 'I'm going for a swim in the sea,' he says. 'Wanna come?'

'How will you get to the sea? We are so high up.'

'I'll show you,' he says, and takes me to the bottom of the garden where there are steep steps that go down to a small private beach inaccessible by any other means.

'What's in the bag?' I ask, as I carefully follow his lead.

'Breadcrumbs for the fish.'

'We're going to feed the fish?'

'Yup.'

He leads the way and at the end of our descent we are standing on a strip of yellow sand that is totally enclosed by rocky cliffs and sea.

He pulls me toward his body and puts a finger under my chin. 'I'm going for a long swim. Can you amuse yourself until I come back?'

'Why can't I come?'

He frowns, instantly worried. 'It will be too far out for you.'

'OK, I'll swim for a bit, and then I'll lie on the beach and wait for you.'

He bends his head and lightly brushes his lips against mine. 'Don't go anywhere.'

I shake my head. 'And leave this paradise?'

He puts the bag into my hand.

'What do I do with the crumbs?'

'Go into the water until you are waist deep and throw a handful.'

'OK.'

He smiles and starts shedding his clothes. He is so fast it is as if he can't wait to get into the water. He takes everything off, and, naked, strides into the waves as I stare at him, bronzed, strong and so perfectly beautiful. When he gets to hip level he raises his hand in a wave and plunges in.

I step in myself. It is so clear it practically compels you to dive into it. When I get waist deep I start throwing handfuls of frozen breadcrumbs. It is a shock to me to see the sudden burst of activity. In seconds all the crumbs are gone. Fascinated I throw another handful and this time I submerge my head to look at them. They are small and silver with black patterns, and utterly beautiful. When all the crumbs are gone I swim for a bit and then I go to lie in the sand. I can see Jake is still swimming out.

I close my eyes and let the sun dry my skin. But after a while I find I am unable to relax. I sit up and I can no longer see him. In a panic I rush to the water's edge. I can just about make him out. My eyes become riveted to his powerful arms as he goes farther and farther out to sea. When he is just a dot on the horizon my throat constricts with fear. What if a really strong current sweeps him away?

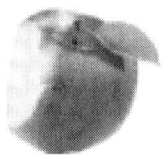

Jake

With every stroke my mind becomes clearer and clearer until it sparkles like crystal. All kinds of scenarios play in my mind. I am sitting at the back of a white transit van, wiping blood from a baseball bat. I am sitting in the dark in someone's apartment and when he comes in and puts on the light he nearly has a heart attack to see me there. And me smiling at him as if he is a long lost friend. That's the thing you learn as a debt collector. People are fuckers—they will cry poverty, until they are threatened with physical violence. Yeah, he paid.

Images of Billy Joe Pilkington come into my mind. His cold, empty eyes. Billy's a legend on his turf. His reputation is one of fearlessness and ruthlessness. His name usually only comes up as a whisper when there is talk of violence and mayhem on the streets, in certain parts of London.

They call him the bat, the bat that came straight out of hell. Nobody has ever dared to cross him. Nobody has dared defy him and lived to tell their story. Nobody except for me. But that was a long time ago when I had nothing to lose.

I know I am *never* going back to that life. It is clear what I need to do. No turf war. Not while I am alive. Carefully, I weigh all the options open to me, all the situations that could arise. Each one of them calls for a true truce. We've had an uneasy truce for too long.

In the distance I can see a yacht. People are sunning themselves on the deck. A woman is standing in a bikini, a hand shading her eyes against the afternoon sun.

She starts waving to me. I stop and turn to look at the beach. I could have gone farther, but I can see Lily standing at the water's edge. I cannot see her face, but I can tell by the tense and fixed way she is standing that she is worried about me. I turn around and start to swim back toward her. As soon as I am standing on the sand she runs to me. She does not say anything, just hugs me tightly.

'I'm so sorry. I'll never put my phone on silent mode again,' she almost sobs.

I lift her out of the water and lay her on the sand. The sea has rejuvenated me but has made her tense and frightened. Her eyes are wide and bright. I place my wet palms on the insides of her thighs—they are warm and gritty with sand—and part them. The sun shines down on us, warming my back. Droplets of sea fall on her face; it is already a lovely shade of gold. Her nipples taste salty when I bite them. She pulls at my hips and screams for more. I force more of me into her. Our coupling is frantic, urgent and wild. There are no sea breezes, but watched by the sea, the sun and the rocks it is the perfect fuck.

Afterwards, we dress and go up the steps hand in hand. I have never felt closer to another human being. Then Dominic calls and I know that once again I will be wiping blood from my body.

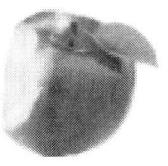

Lily

Evening descends and from every corner night fragrances rise. Every living thing, the grass, the trees, the flowers, the people all bring into the leisure of night their own scent.

And that crowd of odors surrounds us as we sit in the open-air restaurant that Jake has brought me to. I raise my glass of wine and take a sip. It is perfectly chilled. I lick the beads of condensation off the glass. They have their own taste. I look up and he is staring at me. I blush.

'Tell me about your childhood,' I say to cover my sudden gaucheness.

'Until my father...died, I was happy. We never had much money because he was an incurable gambler. I remember that my mother kept debts with everyone, even with the butcher who provided her with the cheapest cuts of meat, but even so we were truly a happy family.'

I look at him with surprise. How accepting he is that his father was a gambler. There is no condemnation, no anger, no feeling that he has been deprived. Only a strange and impressive loyalty to family.

'What about you? What was your childhood like?' he asks.

I had it all down pat—an alcoholic father, a downtrodden mother, everything, the whole shebang, at the tips of my fingers—but I found I couldn't say the words. I didn't want to lie to him! I blinked in surprise. What the hell? I was going to fuck up my first assignment. Make him suspicious.

'I'll tell you about my family another time,' I say, and wanting to distract him I reach out and touch his fingers. Immediately, they move to clasp mine.

I look at our entwined fingers and an old, tired ache of once when I was insane breaks into me and eats at my bones. Its return makes me angry. How pathetic. Sentimental fool. There is no one here I can call my own. This man will never be mine. He will never share my pain. I am here to do a job. I am here to crush him, not to long for him as one does a beloved. I am here to save other people's sons and brothers from dying unnecessarily because of men like him. I look up at him.

'Are you all right?' he asks.

This time I won't allow myself to dissolve in my own grief. This time I will recognize myself. It is simple. It is beautiful. I am not lost. I am strong. I can do this. I smile. Harden my heart and speak.

'I'm fine. You want to know about my family? Let me tell you about them. My father was an alcoholic. I'm not sure if he is still alive. And my mother was a downtrodden, weak woman. She let him beat her and me. When I was fifteen I ran away.'

'I'm sorry,' he says softly, and begins to stroke the inside of my wrist. The movement is gentle and tender, and suddenly I feel like bursting into tears.

'I'm so sorry I asked,' he says.

I look at him. There is an expression of such caring tenderness in his face. Oh, the irony. He thinks I am upset to remember my past. That makes me feel worse. I shake my head. 'It's OK. You said you wanted to come here to think. Have you managed to?'

His eyes darken. 'Yeah, but I'm afraid my plans have been rather turned on their heads.'

'What do you mean?'

'My brother, Dominic, you haven't met him yet, have you?'

I shake my head.

'He's a bit of a hothead. He got drunk and went to one of the Pilkingtons' clubs and challenged Billy Joe Pilkington to a bare knuckle fight.'

'God! But how does a drunken dare affect your plans?'

'Billy Joe Pilkington is an animal. If he fights my brother he will do serious damage to him. I cannot allow that. I am the head of this family

and they are my responsibility. I will fight on behalf of the Eden family. Maybe that will be the end of this silly feud.'

I stare at him aghast. 'That's just barbaric. Nobody fights to settle a dispute anymore. This is the twenty-first century.'

He looks faintly offended, but his voice is calm. 'Bare knuckle fighting is a noble and proud pastime. For us travelers, family is the most important aspect of life. My mother, my brothers and my wife and children when I have them are the most important things in my life. I will do everything in my power to protect them.'

When he says 'my wife' I freeze, my gut constricting with horror. It shocks me to hear him talk about another woman as his wife. The pain is sharper than I can ignore or explain away as a crush or a passing infatuation. How foolish I have been. Of course he will marry some other woman and speak of her possessively. By then I will have ditched all the trappings of this assignment and disappeared into my real life. And then it hits me. Maybe by then he will be behind bars. Because of me.

Because of me this fine man will be behind bars.

And I feel pain in my gut. My body doesn't want me to betray him. 'You are a police officer first and foremost,' Robin's voice says in my head.

I grip the stem of the wine glass and swallow a mouthful. It goes the wrong way and I start

coughing and choking. He comes around and drops to his haunches next to me and asks with great concern if I am all right. I look at him in shock. No other man would do that. They would worry about what other people would think of them. He doesn't care. He honestly couldn't give a shit what anyone else thinks of him. And I clench my hands with rage.

By design this man was made for me, yet I cannot have him.

ELEVEN

I come out of the bathroom and stand in the doorway. He is lying on the bed totally relaxed. The illuminated wall behind the headboard creates an intimate ambience and makes him appear as if he is on a stage. I walk up to him and he opens his eyes slowly and gazes at me, as if he has been dreaming and has woken up to find himself still in the dream. What he has been dreaming of is impossible to say: the expression in his eyes is unfathomable.

His warm hand slides between my thighs. A secret smile plays on his lips. 'Mmmn...' he says. The sound is low, a hum, an invitation.

The hand moves higher.

I take a quick, sharp breath. I am not wearing panties. His fingers touch the wet whorls of flesh, and tendrils of excitement snake across my body. He drags his fingers through the soft, sensitive layers. My head tilts back involuntarily, my eyes half close.

The expression in his eyes changes: gold-green lust shimmers in them.

He pinches the protruding fleshy nub. Quite hard. My eyes widen. He pulls me by my clit toward him. I follow helplessly. He pulls his

knees up so his body makes a seat. Awkwardly, with the most sensitive part of me trapped in his firm grasp, I climb onto his body and sit on his crotch, facing him. His penis is so hard under his clothes it is like sitting on a piece of wood. His eyes are level with my open sex.

'Wider,' he encourages softly.

I comply.

He releases my clit and blood rushes to the numbed flesh making it tingle. For a few seconds he studies the blood-engorged bud while I tremble gently with anticipation. 'For fuck's sake, start,' I want to scream.

He grasps the outer lips of my sex and pulls them apart so the secret, pink inner tissue is exposed, and stares at the glistening flesh. I squirm impatiently. My whole body is hot with desire and excitement. To my disappointment he lets the lips spring closed. His eyes rise up to meet mine.

'Play with yourself.' His voice is thick with need.

I hesitate. I have never done it with someone watching me.

His expression is enigmatic. 'I feel voyeuristic.'

Crystal Jake wants to watch. I take a deep breath. Yeah, sure, you can watch, Jake Eden.

I bring my right hand between my legs and move two fingers in a slow circle around my tingling clit. His eyes drop from my face down to the show between my legs. He watches my actions avidly, greedily. I never thought it would be, but it is an incredible turn-on. I feel dirty, and slutty, and shameless, and absolutely fucking vibrant.

My fingers travel in the familiar practiced movement. I know exactly how I like it. Exactly what makes me come. But there is a different layer this time. He is watching me. It is almost like when he was watching me dance. I feel powerful. Desired. Wanted. I close my eyes, my hips lifting, my muscles tightening. Small moans of pleasure escape from my lips as I welcome that gathering knot, the bunching muscles, the promise of an impending orgasm. I am so close to my climax… Almost there.

'Yes, yes,' I breathe.

Then his hot hand closes over mine.

I open my eyes and stare at him, needy and frustrated. Knowing. He is not going to let me come.

'No,' he says softly, and inserting two fingers into me, orders, 'Take your top off.'

With his fingers impaled deep inside me I hurriedly pull my top off, my movements clumsy. I am not wearing a bra and his eyes latch onto my naked breasts.

'Come closer,' he says, in the kind of deep, seductive voice that I have always imagined the big bad wolf using on Red Riding Hood.

Oh, Mr. Wolf, how long I have waited for you.

I lay my palms on either side of him and lean forward until my back is arched like a bow and my breasts are almost brushing his lips. He captures one swollen nipple in his mouth and swirls his tongue around it.

''Yes,' I encourage.

He starts sucking the tip gently and with such a soft mouth that I groan. Shockwaves of pure pleasure course through me.

'Offer me the other,' he commands.

With unseemly haste I fit the other tip into his warm, wet mouth. So gentle. The way I imagine a toothless baby would take a nourishing nipple. I let out a long breath of satisfaction and start grinding my sex against the heel of his palm. He lets me until the tremors begin shaking my whole body, and it is clear that I'm going to climax. Then he pulls his hand away and catches my nipple between his teeth. I look at him. I am almost screaming with frustration and the sadistic fucker is enjoying this.

'Let me come, damn you,' I groan.

He lets go of my nipple and smiles slowly. 'Persuade me.'

'There is this,' I say, and lifting my hips away from his crotch, I unzip his trousers. His erection is straining against the waistband of his boxers.

'That's the most persuasive argument I've heard all day,' he says.

'Wait till you hear the rest of my argument.' I slide my hand around his shaft and it swells even more.

'Can't wait,' he mutters.

'Get your knees down,' I order suddenly.

 73

His eyes flash at my strict tone, but his voice is even: 'Done.' He flattens his legs.

I lift myself off him and on my knees walk along his body up to his face and then carefully turn around so I am facing his feet. I lower my sex until it is suspended a few tantalizing inches away from his mouth.

'Smell me,' I command. I hold still while he lifts his head and sniffs me. I know what is coming next. And it does. His tongue flicks out. I allow one lick. It makes me shiver with pleasure. The desire to let him carry on is immense, but I control myself.

'Who told you to lick me?' I ask sternly, and lift my hips away from his mouth. 'You've ruined it. You'll just have to wait until tomorrow now.'

He moves so fast I register the sound of his muffled laughter before I realize I am immovably trapped between two hard hands around my hips.

'You wait till tomorrow if you want to. I'm having you tonight,' he growls and suddenly I am sprawled awkwardly on his body with my legs spread, my pussy opened on his mouth, and his tongue thrust into me.

'Hey, I'm supposed to be in charge,' I protest as I try to push myself up on my hands.

'Cock teasers don't get to be in charge.'

His hand comes down around my waist to force me down while the other slips underneath my body. His fingers work my clit in exactly the way he learned from me earlier. In that exposed,

helpless position, him devouring my pussy, and his fingers doing exactly what I love to my nub, my orgasm comes so fast and so hard, my nails claw into his thighs.

When it is all over, I find myself lying with my cheek on his belly and panting hard while he is still sucking my swollen folds softly. It's very, very delicious and unspeakably decadent, but I lift my cheek, turn my head, and find myself looking at a very beautifully decorated, very erect throbbing penis. Clear liquid is running down it.

On my belly I shimmy toward it and extending my tongue follow the body of the snake all the way to its open mouth.

'Oh yeah,' he encourages hoarsely.

With my lips held in a tight pout, slowly, inch by hot inch I swallow that deliciously bulbous apple, and then as much of that thick and twisting snake as I can. I bob my head faster and faster, not even stopping when I feel one long finger slide into me. It occurs to me then—the kind of view he must have of my open pussy with its gaping, glistening hole begging to be penetrated. I squirm encouragingly and he fits another finger in and starts pumping into me while I suck him as furiously and as fast as I can.

Suddenly, he grabs me by the waist and pulls me off his shaft. My mouth comes off with a wet, slurping sound. Before I can say Jake Eden I am put on my hands and knees. Threading his fingers into my hair, he pulls my head back, as he rams into me.

'Ahh…' I scream, my head jerking back.

'That's what I was missing. Watching my cock disappear into you,' he says, pushing himself in so hard I shudder.

He fucks me harder and harder, forcing his cock deeper and deeper, and I start to feel the verge of another climax.

'Yesssss…' I push into him, my muscles clenching and tightening as we climb the heights together.

He wakes me up in the night.

'Want to go for a midnight swim?'

It is too dark to see his expression, only the bulk of his naked shoulder, the way it rises out of bed, strong and full of power. 'Yes,' I whisper.

We pad down to the swimming pool. He dives in. I dip a toe in. The water is cold. But it is OK. Under the stars we swim together like two carefree eels, sparks flying whenever we touch. Later his body is warm as it moves on top of me.

TWELVE

I wake up alone and touch the indent on the pillow where his head has been. Then I roll over to his side and bury my nose in the scent of his shampoo.

'Oh, Jake,' I whisper.

I get out of the bed and walk to the living room. The house is very quiet. For a while I think he has gone out and then I know where he is. The sliding doors are open. I walk around the swimming pool and stand at the edge of the cliff and far away in the ocean, much farther than he went yesterday, I see him, swimming furiously. He only came back yesterday because of me.

Once again, I am beset by gnawing fear and worry.

I go into the kitchen and open the freezer door. Other than a couple of trays of ice it is filled with bags of breadcrumbs. I take a bag and go down the steps. I go into the water and feed the fish. I watch them as they frantically snatch at the crumbs and it is a beautiful thing, but I feel restless and distracted. Suddenly, impulsively, I decide to swim out to him. I know I won't be able to swim that far, but perhaps I can meet him halfway on his return.

I strike out toward him. I must have been swimming for a good ten minutes, and yet he seems even farther away. I realize that I am already very tired. I stop and start treading water. I look back at the shore. It looks dauntingly far. It was a stupid idea.

I holler out to Jake, but my voice doesn't carry. I have a little moment of panic. Suddenly, as if he has somehow felt my distress, he stops, turns, sees me, and immediately begins swimming powerfully toward me. I tread water and watch. He is a fine swimmer, sleek and fast. He dives under and pops up in front of me, water sluicing down his hair and face, as ageless and as at home in the sea as a seal.

His eyes are thunderous. 'What the fuck are you doing so far from the beach?' he demands furiously.

I feel stung by his anger. He has never spoken like that to me before. I stare at him in astonishment.

'Don't you know how fucking dangerous it is?' he snarls.

'Fuck off,' I spit at him, and begin to swim toward the beach. He grabs me from behind. His body is hard and slippery.

It is a relief to stop kicking and simply relax into his body.

He nuzzles my neck, his breath warm. 'Can you make it back on your own?'

'No,' I admit reluctantly.

He catches me under my arms, and slowly we make it back to shore.

We lay at the water's edge, naked. I look up at the wonderfully blue sky and feel the heat of the sun penetrating my skin. 'It was a stupid thing to do, I'm sorry.'

He turns his head and our eyes meet. In the sunlight they are bright and intense, dizzying: the color of spring grass. His eyelashes are all long and dark and stuck together with seawater, like a child that has been crying. 'I'm sorry I shouted at you, Lil. But you scared me.' He blinks. 'If anything had happened to you, I would have been too far out to do anything to help you.'

I raise my hand and lay it on his flat stomach. He takes his hand and traces my mouth and desire starts to stain his eyes. He moves forward and leans his forehead on my shoulder and takes a deep shuddering breath. 'Oh, Lil. What am I going to do with you?'

I wriggle myself so I am underneath his body, sweat seeping into my skin. 'I have an idea,' I say, focusing on his brutally masculine chest.

He looks down on me. A hint of that which is centuries old, plain ol' human lust, shines in his face. Fire explodes in my skull. I am so addicted to this man.

'I really like the way you think.' His amused whisper slides into my head like a little mind trick.

Some may call it love. I don't.

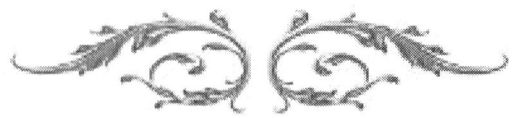

'Hungry?' I ask.

'Starving.'

We toss a coin to decide who is to make breakfast. He loses and to ease the pain I promise to make dinner. I stand against the counter and watch him put a pan on the stove.

'Who taught you to cook?'

He smiles, cheeky. 'Let's get something straight, Lil. I don't cook. I'm frying a couple of eggs because I lost a coin toss.'

I can't help smiling back. Like this he is pure magic. The twinkling of his eyes warms my heart the way standing next to a three bar heater in a freezing room in winter warms the body. It actually makes me want to kiss that sexy mouth.

'You don't smile very often, do you?' I say.

'No?'

'No.' I look at him from beneath my lashes. 'What would make you smile right now?'

An inscrutable expression crosses his eyes then is gone as quickly as it came. Then he smiles suddenly, dashing and irresistible. The pull of it is undeniable. I feel my knees weaken.

'How's that?' he asks.

'Not bad, considering how out of practice you are,' I tease.

He steps closer and taking my shoulders in his hand, lowers his mouth to mine. The power of the unexpected kiss is shocking. It whips through me, setting fire to my senses. I hear the roaring in my ears as my mouth opens. He draws me closer and my whole body presses into his hard, clear need, and gives without questioning. My body knows what I refuse to acknowledge: I need him. I open my eyes quickly.

'I'll make the toast,' I squeak, and walk unsteadily away to put some slices of bread into the toaster.

We have breakfast on the terrace and I eat with relish. I wipe my plate clean with a piece of toast and grin at him. 'That was delicious, thank you.'

He leans back in his chair and smiles, beautiful eyes flashing. 'So, my little wildcat, how would you like to take a tour of the island?'

I let my gaze travel over him, cool. 'You know all my buttons.'

'Good. Because I'm trying to impress you here.'

'You're doing great so far.'

He rises and holds out his hand.

Putting a sway into my hips, I walk with him through the house into the garage. He hits the button that opens the outside garage door and pulls a plastic cover off an absolutely stunning red and black Ducati Multistrada.

'Wow! This is some bike,' I exclaim walking around it, my sway forgotten. It is so spanking new there is not a scratch on it. I look at him, impressed.

He is beaming like a child. 'Great, isn't she?'

'Awesome.'

'Come on,' he says, throwing his leg over the machine.

'What? You're going to go like that!' He is wearing the same faded jeans, old sneakers and nothing else.

'Why not?'

'No helmet?'

'Ah, Lil. Do you really need the government to be your nanny and tell you what to wear all the fucking time?'

'What if we meet with an accident?'

He sighs. 'There's a helmet in the cupboard.'

He kicks the bike over and it roars dangerously into life the way a really good bike should. The smell of exhaust fumes fills the garage. He turns to look at me as I fit the helmet on my head.

He winks at me and I gingerly swing my leg over the seat of the bike and place my feet on the passenger pegs.

'Hold me tight,' he says.

I scoot forward until my body is leaning against his and wrap my arms around his hard midsection.

'Ready?'

'Ready.'

He takes off and as he leaves the driveway and gets on the road he accelerates and I hold tighter. He rides with precision and skill as if the bike is an extension of him. When he dips I follow. We cruise along the open road, the wind in our faces, my body glued to his. We travel downhill through the labyrinth of cobbled lanes and make for the roads lined with pines, almond trees and juniper bushes that hug the coastline. Ibiza is full of goats, picturesque coves, tall rocky cliffs, lovely beaches and old-fashioned boatsheds made of wood. Contrary to what I believe about the island being the playground of celebrities and fashion models, so much of it is green and undeveloped. We pass a lonely, whitewashed, hilltop church and at the end of it an olive grove starts. I tap Jake's shoulder and shout over the roar of the bike for him to stop. He slows down and pulls up at the edge of the road then cuts the engine.

'What?' he says, turning to me, his hair wind-blown, his cheeks flushed.

The whole time the tips of my breasts encased only in the thin bikini top have been rubbing against his naked back and I am feeling unbelievably horny.

'I want you,' I say, and taking my helmet off I get off the bike and walk into the grove.

By the time he comes for me I am lying naked on the hot orange soil, my legs spread. When his hard cock enters me, his eyes raping me, raking over my exposed body like rough hands, I hiss with relief.

THIRTEEN

Jake

From the open door I watch her wash vegetables in the sink. She turns off the tap and reaches for a knife. Her hair falls forward and she flicks it away carelessly. The gesture arrests me. Compels me to stay and watch. It is as if I am watching a movie. She is someone else. I am someone else. The picture of domestic bliss is so foreign. So alluring. It warms my heart.

What is it about her that makes her so magnetic? Even the simplest thing she does becomes a movement of grace and beauty. I have to stop myself from going into the kitchen, lifting her onto the counter and fucking her until she claws at me.

She leaves the tap running and turns to check on a pan of boiling water. As she puts the lid back on it she looks in my direction, sees me, and for an instant loses her concentration. The lid slips from her hand and falls to the ground, catching a ladle resting by the side of the pan on its way. The ladle pings up and falls into the pan of boiling water and splashes boiling water onto her hand.

I hear the ladle clatter to the floor as I rush to her and try to pull her toward the cold water tap, but she shakes her head vehemently.

'Flour,' she gasps. 'Find me some flour.'

I stare at her, confounded; convinced I have heard her wrong. 'What?'

'Where's the flour?' she barks urgently.

Flour! As if I would know where that is. I start opening cupboards and clumsily rifle through them. Dropping packets on the counter and floor. Cursing. I find an unopened packet in the third cupboard I open. I turn around quickly,

'Open it,' she instructs, white with pain.

I open it and pass it to her. She takes a handful of flour and holding it against her burn, closes her eyes. It must have given her some relief because she looks up at me and smiles tremulously.

'I know it looks weird but it's an old Chinese trick my grandmother taught me. She actually keeps a packet of corn flour in the fridge so it is cold and ready for use whenever she burns herself.'

I stare at her in shock. This is the first time she has offered a tiny little snippet of herself, without being prompted, and something real!

'It's brilliant,' she adds. 'It actually helps heal the burn faster and stops the skin from marking.'

I keep my voice casual. 'Your grandmother is Chinese?'

She smiles. A tender expression comes into her eyes. 'Yes.'

'And you love her very much, don't you?'

'Yes, yes I do.'

'And she is still alive?'

Suddenly the expression in her eyes changes, becomes guarded and fearful. And all I want to do is hold her close to me and tell her it doesn't matter. It does not matter a damn. She has ruined nothing by telling me that.

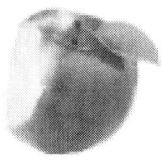

Lily

I stare at him in horror. Oh! My! God! I have totally slipped out of character. My alter ego doesn't even remember her grandparents. I can't believe I have fucked up so bad. What if he wants to know more about her? Or, worse, wants to meet her? I can't tell him she is dead. I think of her, her head tipped back, roaring with laughter. My grandmother is very superstitious—Chinese believe all mention of death and dying is bad luck, and she would be so hurt if she knew I was telling anyone she was dead. I'll have to tell Mills and the agency will have to come up with a fake grandmother. But that will be embarrassing, too. Admitting that I slipped up this early in the assignment.

I drop my eyes to my hand.

'How long do you have to do that for?' he asks.

I put my head up and see him looking at the flour I am holding against my burn.

'Ten minutes.' The flour has helped, but it is still painful.

He switches the fire off. 'Come on,' he says, and with his hand on the small of my back leads me toward the living room. 'We'll order in tonight.'

To my great relief he loses interest in my grandmother and does not ask anything else about her.

It will be our last night on the island. Some part of me doesn't want to leave. I have been happy here. Happier than I have ever been in my life. We have watched the sunset over the water and had our takeaway pizza, and now Jake has gone in to have a shower.

I stand on the terrace for a little while longer soaking in the magic of the island. A lizard scampers up a tree. I know a faint tinge of envy. It lives in this paradise. I watch it until it disappears into some bushes. With a sigh I go indoors and pull out a book from my bag. Curling up on the sofa I start to read. Three pages later Jake is standing in the doorway.

'Hey,' he says.

I gaze at him. He is wearing a pair of faded jeans. They hug his strong thighs. Something about him always makes my mouth dry. 'Hey, yourself,' I reply.

'What are you reading?'

'*The Billionaire Banker*.'

'Any good?'

'Not bad.'

He comes forward, the muscles of his chest gleaming in the down-lights. Desire floods through me, so hot and fast that my clit aches.

I pat the sofa next to me.

He raises his eyebrows.

'I want to try something.'

His eyebrows rise. 'What?'

I turn my book to the appropriate page and hand it over to him. 'I want to try that.'

He takes the book from me and reads. I watch him, the way the light caresses his cheekbones, the shadows his long eyelashes make, the straight mouth. A beautiful man, a truly beautiful man. When he looks up his eyes are dark and amused. 'I've got whiskey.'

'I know where I can get some ice,' I say with a grin.

By the time I come back with a bucket of ice, he has stripped naked. His big thighs are bunched and ready and his decorated, satiny soft cock is erect and magnificent in the soft glow of the lights. He is so hot and so perfect my thighs quiver. In one hand he is holding a bottle of Jack Daniel's.

I lean weakly against a pillar. 'Already so hard?'

He doesn't answer. Instead he opens me with his practiced fingers and does to me what the billionaire banker did to his woman.

FOURTEEN

The first thing I do at work when I return from our little holiday is go on the Internet and find out about bare knuckle fighting, a sport where the opponents ram their unprotected fists into each other to decide who is the hardest of them. What I discover scares the shit out of me.

The activity is considered to be the ultimate tear-up, no fucking around, no holds barred and with plenty of blood. It could be pouring from a fighter's ears or even from his groin, bitten by his opponent.

I also learn that the impact of one man's bare fist on another is equivalent to the force of a four pound lump hammer traveling at twenty miles an hour. The effect could be devastating, even after a bout lasting just a few minutes. There are no official rounds to this blood sport; instead it just goes on until one of them cannot take it anymore, or has sustained so many injuries that he can no longer stand.

It reminds me of the Chinese proverb my grandmother used to tell us grandchildren: *When two tigers fight, one limps away horribly wounded, the other is dead.*

That evening, profoundly disturbed and unable to wait, I run to the front door as soon as I hear Jake enter and confront him. 'Is it true that in bare knuckle fighting you could be bitten so hard in the groin that you start bleeding?' I demand.

He closes the door with a deliberate click. 'It won't be like that, Lil. Both Pilkington and I are too proud to bite like wild animals.'

I clasp my hands together nervously. 'But you could end up with a broken eye socket or a smashed fist?' The thought makes me tremble.

'Unlikely. The fight will be marshaled by a referee.'

'But the possibility exists that you could get hurt?' I insist.

'Yes, I could,' he admits.

I take a deep breath. 'And what happens when you do?'

'There will be a paramedic on standby.'

'It says on the Internet that you could be brain damaged. What could a paramedic do then?' I cry.

'I could die tomorrow crossing the street.'

'I don't want you to fight,' I blurt out unhappily.

He takes my trembling hands in his, but looks at me with an unyielding face. 'It is tragic, but we both have to go through this fight simply to sustain our identities. I *have* to fight him, Lil. It is all arranged. The date has been set. Saturday coming. And there is no backing out.'

I gasp. 'And when were you going to tell me that?'

'Saturday.'

Angrily I pull my hands out of his grasp. 'Before or after the fight?'

He runs his fingers through his hair. 'Before. I was trying to avoid a scene like this.'

'Where will it be held?' I ask coldly.

'In a barn somewhere.'

'I hope you've reserved a good seat for me,' I throw at him sarcastically.

'You're not going.'

My eyes widen. 'Why can't I go?'

He folds his arms over his chest. 'Do you really want to watch two men inflict savage injuries on each other?'

I narrow my eyes. 'I thought you said the injuries are not going to be savage?'

He frowns. 'Just stop it, Lil. You're not coming, OK?'

'It's a spectator sport so won't there be others there, including women?'

'Yes.' His voice is cautious.

'And you said it is a noble tradition.'

'Yes.'

'Well, I want to be with you while you engage in this noble tradition.'

'Well, I don't want you there.'

'Why not?'

'Because I will be distracted and unable to concentrate if you are. I want to know that you are in a safe place. *At home.*'

Some part of me is relieved to know that I am not going to see the fight. It makes me sick to even watch a boxing fight between total strangers. I don't know that I can take watching Jake bloodied in such a barbaric way. 'Will you at least let me come and wait in the car for you?'

He sighs. 'All right, you can wait in the car with Shane.'

I look at him. 'Will many people be going?'

'Entrance is by word of mouth and the location will only be revealed a few hours earlier by the organizers, so nobody really knows how many will turn up until the day.'

'Will people be betting?'

He shrugs. 'They usually do.'

Saturday flies into my life. Nobody talks and I sit in the back of the car, sullen and fearful, as Shane drives us to a barn in the middle of nowhere. Dominic has gone on ahead and will meet us at the location of the fight.

A swarthy boy is directing cars down a beaten track to a field. I am shocked to see what looks like hundreds of cars parked there. Shane passes them and comes to a stop outside a barn. There is a van selling hot dogs and burgers. As I watch, people are going into the barn.

Dominic has been waiting for us to arrive. He comes striding toward us. He is tall and broad like his brothers, but it is immediately apparent that he is not the thinker of the family.

'It's a fucking zoo in there,' he says bending down at Jake's window.

'Is Pilkington here yet?' Jake asks.

'Just arrived. He's got a lot of supporters. His women are going crazy, but don't worry, it won't take you long to put him to sleep.'

Jake gets out of the car. I scramble out, too. Dominic acknowledges me with a nod. I don't nod back. I know it is him that has caused this fight.

Jake turns toward me and smiles. 'Kiss me good luck?'

I fling myself at him and, holding the sides of his face between my palms, I kiss him desperately. His mouth is warm. His hands come around my waist. And his tongue traces my teeth gently. But there is no passion. There is only the sense of cold fingers crawling all over me. I break away. He smiles again at me.

Shane comes around to stand beside me as I watch Jake stride away with Dom.

Close to the barn, he stops, and turns around to look at us. I wave at him, but he simply stares at me as if this could be the last time he will see me. The thought makes my throat constrict with

fear. What if something happens to him? Brain damage. Or...death. People have died during these fights.

The thought galvanizes me, and I take a step to run toward him, but Shane's arm shoots out and grasps my forearm. I stop and do not move. He holds me still while Jake carries on staring at me.

Finally, Jake nods and, turning away, walks into the barn. He never turns again. He enters the door and I hear the crowds roar their welcome. I feel a shiver go through me. Shane removes his hand. I hug myself. I don't want to think of what is going on in that barn.

I turn my head to look at Shane. He is staring at the entrance, his face tense and anxious.

'It's going to be OK, right?'

'Yeah, it's going to be OK,' he says very softly, not looking at me.

This is the first time I have been alone with him since that night at the party when he found Jake with his fingers inside me. 'I'm sorry,' I say.

His head whips around. 'About what?'

'About that night. I didn't mean to hurt you or cause trouble between you and Jake.'

He stares at me incredulously. 'You don't understand at all, do you?'

'Understand what?'

'My brother would never have done that if you were right for me.'

I stare at him curiously. This unshakeable loyalty they all have toward each other even at their own expense.

'My brother is the father I never had. Did you know that his burning ambition was to be a vet? He wanted to be the best vet in the world. He was convinced he could talk to animals. Maybe he could. Even fierce dogs used to wag their tails at him.'

His eyes harden.

'He gave it all up for us. We are what we are today because of him, because he took the tough decisions and did whatever was necessary for us to stay alive and thrive. I owe my life to him. So yes, I liked you, but contrary to what you think, I had no problems stepping aside. And I am proud that I did something for him. I introduced him to you.'

I flush bright red with guilt. 'I'm not special,' I mumble.

'You're so clever and yet so blind,' he says, shaking his head. 'When you see him, what do you see?'

I shake my head. My thoughts about Jake are so jumbled, so conflicted and so confused that even I have not tried to analyze them yet.

'You see a flashy criminal, don't you? He dresses that way because those are the trappings of those he deals with and it is a disguise he wears so they do not see that he is not one of them.'

I think of Jake on the horse and the way he was when we were alone on the island. He was most comfortable when he was unshaven, barefoot and shirtless.

'Do you really think my brother treats *anyone else* the way he treats you? I've never seen a woman get as close as you have to him. In fact, to my knowledge no one has. Don't fuck it up by mistaking the strong emotions he has for you with weakness.'

FIFTEEN

Jake

The atmosphere in the barn is buzzing. All around me side bets and cash seem to be changing hands. Dominic has rounded up some of our boys to shout their welcome for me, but they are few compared to the people who have come to see The Bat.

At six feet two, an inch shorter than me, but weighing well over nineteen stones, and with a chest that is reported to be fifty-five inches, he is not just a veteran of at least thirty bare-knuckle fights, but a champion, too. I made light of it to Lily, but Billy Joe Pilkington has never lost a fight. His opponents are known to be either out cold or crawling pathetically away from him at the end of the fight.

And now he believes no one can beat him.

Taking a deep breath I walk toward the makeshift ring. It's been so long since I have been in one. The ring is a claustrophobically small six by six feet square made of three bales of hay stacked up to mid-thigh level. Billy Joe stands in one corner, shirtless, his chest puffed out and covered in tattoos, the largest being a bat with its mouth open in a red scream, and the letters No Fear written in olde English font.

His eyes, black with cold intent, are fixed on me, as he pulls a mouthful of Guinness from a can. He swallows and slowly and deliberately clenches his fist. White frothy liquid shoots out of the can and pours over his large hand. He flings the crushed bit of metal aside and, with a savage roar, repeatedly bangs his chest with his fist in an astonishing show of bad ass.

Staring at me he punches his fist—one of the knuckles has been smashed to smithereens during a fight—into his open palm. He's getting off on the adoration of the crowd and trying to intimidate me.

I step over the cordon of hay and I am in the ring with Pilkington.

I feel the eyes of every single person in that packed barn. All hoping to spot a telltale weakness, a slight twitch, a nervous smile, a dropping of the eyelids. Any small sign to decide which corner to put their money in. But I keep my attention totally focused on Pilkington. He is much bigger than I remember, stronger, and more muscular. There is a new scar on his face. It looks like a bite mark.

In that moment I realize we are two different species. He's fighting to die and I'm fighting to live. This is totally against everything I am supposed to be doing with my life. Nevertheless, this fight is real and it is happening. For a second my mind shifts to Lily waiting outside. I push the thought away. Shane is watching over her. She is safe. I need to get this done. I train my thoughts back to my adversary.

'What you waiting for, Eden?' Pilkington taunts.

His voice inspires an instant eruption from the crowd. They jeer and bay for blood. Anyone's will do, it's all part of the bare-knuckle sport!

Pilkington takes a step forward into my space and I take one into his. I meet him glare for glare. We are so close our noses are practically touching. This is as primeval as it gets. Two rivals locking horns in a battle for supremacy.

His raging black eyes blink, and suddenly he head-butts me and swings a thunderous right my way. I register the breeze that slithers up my cheek as his iron knuckles swish by and hear the sickening crack of his fist connecting with my temple, before my brain rattles in my head and my ears start ringing. My legs give way under me and I go crashing to the ground. But I am so hyped up and racing with adrenalin I don't feel the pain. All around me his supporters are going crazy.

'Do him. Fucking do him,' they howl.

This is a bad start. I know that he already has one on me.

Every punch takes a little out of me. It isn't like it is on TV. It's exhausting. Unfortunately for Billy Pilkington, though, we're not yet half an hour into the battle when I'll be weaker. His blow disorientates me only momentarily. I look up and see him, feet apart, hands raised, as if he is a conquering gladiator who has already delivered the final blow. Boy is he wrong. I'm not done. Not by a long shot.

'Come on, Jake,' Dominic screams somewhere from my left.

I shake my head to clear it and get to my feet. This time Pilkington doesn't have surprise on his side. I explode forward with a powerful uppercut. He leans backward to evade it, and I kick him. He staggers, but stays upright.

I throw a punch into the side of his jaw. He ducks, and I land a solid blow to his liver. The pain causes air to whoosh out of his lungs. He retaliates with a blow to my left kidney. I gasp with the flash of pain and land on my knees. Fuck that hurt. I'm gonna be pissing blood for the next few days.

I scramble up, but he sideswipes my legs from underneath me. I topple backwards. He staggers toward me, and with a furious screech, throws himself on top of me. The weight of him landing on me is unreal. My body jerks. His large hand spiders across my face and digs into my eyes. I slam my elbow into his ribs, and hear the crack of bone. His eyes widen. He rolls off me.

We are both on our feet.

I unleash a powerful uppercut down the middle that catches him on the chin. Whack. He grimaces and falls with a dull thud, almost as if he's unconscious before he even hits the floor. For one moment I think it's done, but the next thing I see, he is sitting up, blood spilling from his mouth, and what the fuck? Smiling at me. Well, that's a fucking first, no one's ever got up without help from my best shot. That shot should have dropped a horse.

I realize single punches are not going to crack this tough nut as I watch him get back on his feet and turn to face me. With a grunt he takes a lurching step forward. The odd move disarms me. He swings out and connects heavily with my ribs. A searing flash of pain ripples through my torso.

Winded, I double over, and stagger back unsteadily. The punch has the effect of knocking in the backs of my knees. My head is swimming, but blindly I hit out for his body.

I know I'm in a fucking war when a left body shot opens me up to a pair of knuckles that feel like they're encased in steel. My head snaps around from the unbelievable force. My mouth fills with blood. I swallow a mouthful and, protecting my head, fire back, unleashing multiple combinations that rain down on him.

His head looks like it might come off his shoulders. Fuck knows how he's staying on his feet. One thing I got to say for him, he is as strong as a damn bull. He keeps coming forward throwing bombs. One lands hard on my jaw. I see a vapor mist of my blood spray the onlookers. It makes them yell louder. The more blood the better, just so long as it isn't theirs.

I suck up the pain and catch him again, this time with a devastating blow to the solar plexus that bends him in two. I watch him drop to his knees, face etched in pain, blood pouring from his mouth and a gaping eye cut. He's a fucking mess, but the fucker won't stay down.

I gulp some air as he staggers toward me, and I remember the hard way what I've learned with fighters—no matter how exhausted your opponent is, the last thing to go is the power of his punch—when a crunching punch lands on my ribs followed by an exploding right to my jaw. It sends more blood spraying all over two guys closest to me. The impact of the rib shot sends me winded to the floor. I choke and cough violently.

'Fucking give it up, Eden,' Pilkington bellows, swaying over me, his face snarled and bloodied.

But quitting is not in my genes. I can take his best dogs. I get to my feet—it is only adrenalin that is keeping me going now—and start dancing the famous Eden shuffle. It's been so long, but it comes back to me as clear as if it was yesterday. It mesmerizes and dazes Pilkington. My jabs come from every angle making his life a little worse with every shot. They're too fast for him to see them coming out of that swollen eye of his and he's too fatigued to block any.

The sustained assault on his face and body leaves him gasping for breath. I watch him finally

wilt and collapse after three more hard blows. The crowd becomes frenzied: they know as do I. He won't throw another punch. He's done. He's not the only one—the earlier strength in my legs deserts me and I slither to the ground beside him, blood and sweat dripping from my body.

We've neither won.

The referee will have to decide on points.

But before he can make his decision, a decision that could start another feud, the barn is split by the sound of a man's voice screaming, 'Police, police.'

The lookout has spotted them a mile away, which gives us a few minutes to get out of here. The two hundred odd people in this warehouse panic and start running for the exit in a mass exodus.

Dom and another man are beside me. 'We got to go,' Dom says.

'Wait.'

I turn my head and Pilkington's heavies are trying to help him up. I grab his upper arm. Pain shoots through my ribs. His mouth spills a long cable of saliva, his face is split and bruised, his hair and clothing are slathered in blood, grease and mud. He looks like a wild man. We both look like wild men, blindsided by lightning.

'It's over between us,' I squeeze forcefully, and he just looks at me. His eyes are no longer electric, replaced by the aftermath mellowness of a punishing battle.

'I respect you, Jake Eden,' he says, and a spray of blood hits my face. 'You have fucking balls. You met me head on. Your family and mine are tight now. You won't have any trouble from the Pilkingtons.'

I stick out my bleeding hand. He takes it. Like a man.

'You're one tough fuck, Billy Joe Pilkington, and I wouldn't want to do that again.' He breaks into painful laughter that makes him wince. A mutual rush of respect flows through me.

In typically modest fashion he says, 'You're the greatest fighter of all time… Next to me.'

I grin.

I hear the sirens now. His men slide their hands under his armpits and help him away.

In a daze, I hear a woman's voice calling me frantically. Ah, Lily.

And then I see her face. God! She looks like a fucking angel.

SIXTEEN

Lily

'Oh, my God, Jake! You're covered in blood,' I scream, falling to the ground next to him. I cannot believe the state he is in.

'Have you seen the other guy?' he jokes, blood dribbling out of his mouth.

I stare at him in horror.

'Come on,' Dom shouts urgently. 'We better get the fuck out of here. In a few minutes the pigs will be swarming all over this place.'

'Shane's waiting in the front with the engine running,' I say automatically, remembering what Shane had told me. The sirens sound a whole lot closer. 'Come on,' I say, my voice high and shrill. 'We have to hurry.'

Pilkington's men rush forward to grab an arm each. By a weird chance my gaze collides with one of his helpers and the man's eyes register recognition before he moves his eyes swiftly away. But I have never seen him in my life. Then they are making for the exit and I turn my attention back to Jake, with all my thoughts back to the worry of getting Jake into Shane's car before the police arrive.

Dom and another guy support Jake. It is shocking that in his state he can still walk. I run ahead to open the back door of the car. Jake is put in, Dom and the guy run off, and Shane takes off. The sirens are deafening now, but the coppers are about to find that they're too late again. It is shocking how quickly all the cars have sped away.

I turn to look at Jake.

'Oh my, Jake. Look at you,' I whisper.

'Most of this blood is not mine,' he lies.

'We're going to see a doctor, right?'

'Nope. A doctor is coming to see us.'

I lean back and close my eyes. I feel shocked and shaken.

'Hey,' he says.

I turn my head.

'The feud is over.'

I nod sadly. The price seems too high to me. 'Are you in agony?'

'No, I'm still buzzing.'

'Buzzing?'

'Yup. Buzzing. It's up there with sex.'

I raise my eyebrows.

'Maybe not,' he grins, then winces with pain.

I look at him worriedly and he touches my face gently. And for some crazy reason tears start slipping from my eyes.

'Don't, Lil. Don't. *Everything* is just the way it should be.'

'It's just the shock,' I sniff. Even I don't know why I am crying. It seems so silly, but I feel unbelievably choked up and shaken.

We hurtle through country lanes, with Jake wincing now and again.

The doctor comes and to my horror tells us that Jake has fractured ribs. He prescribes a course of anti-inflammatory meds and painkillers. I set up an ice bath and Jake gingerly lowers himself into it. The buzz of adrenalin has worn off and the damaged ribs make even talking an incredibly painful thing. He lies in the ice bath for about an hour. I can see huge purple bruises and bumps coming up on his legs, his midsection and his face.

'How do you feel?' I ask, coming to sit on the toilet seat.

'Like hell. Even breathing makes me feel miserable. And I've got a splitting headache.'

When he gets out of his ice bath, he is shivering and I gently help him to bed and cover him with a blanket. Then I wrap his hands with gauze bandages—the skin over the knuckles is all broken and raw.

'Why don't you have a little nap?' I say.

He sighs. 'I'd like to have sex.'

I look at him in astonishment. 'How?'

'I could if you did all the work.'

I shake my head in wonder. He can't even breathe without pain and he wants to have sex. Incredible!

'Will you?' he cajoles.

'No. Look at the state of you. Your face looks like a damn balloon. And you can't even breathe properly. I'm not going to have sex with you. What if I cause you even more injuries?'

'We haven't had sex in three days,' he says sulkily.

'And whose fault is that? Who had to conserve energy to prepare for his big fight?'

'How about a blow job?'

'You're mad.'

'I thought you liked a swollen cock.'

I grin. 'I'm not doing it.'

'Right then, just open your legs and let me see your pussy.'

I blush.

'Right, at least just talk dirty to me.'

'Stop it, Jake. I'm not doing anything like that. You're supposed to be resting.'

'Go on. I just want to see my cock in your pretty mouth.'

I lift the duvet and fucking hell he is as hard as a piece of wood. I lay the duvet back on his body.

'Spoilsport,' he grumbles.

I grin.

'By the way, we have to go see my mother in a few days' time. She wants to meet you.'

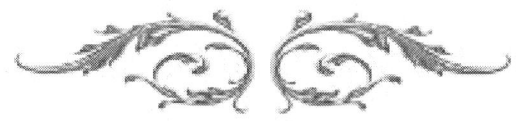

'Wake up, Lily. Wake up.' Jake's voice startles me awake. Disorientated, there is still a great rage left over from my dream. I turn to look at him in the light from his bedside table. He is too stiff and in pain to move too much and is lying on his back looking at me with worried eyes.

He reaches out and pulls me gently backwards onto the pillow. 'You were shouting.'

My skin is damp with sweat. I inhale deeply. 'Can't you sleep?'

'It hurts to sleep.' His voice is dry.

I rise up on one elbow. 'Is the pain really bad?'

'I'll live. Are *you* all right, Lil?'

I take a deep, calming breath. 'It was nothing. Just a nightmare.'

'What was it about?'

The hole that cannot be filled yawns. I can't tell him about Luke. There is only one way I

know to distract him. I give a tiny laugh. 'Do you still want to have sex?'

For a second he seems confused, and then I see that familiar gleam of sexual arousal flickering in the depths of his eyes. 'What do you think?'

I lift the duvet off our bodies and then I place both my palms on either side of him, very, very gently lowering myself onto his erect cock, sighing with pleasure as that big cock invades, stretches and fills me.

'God! I've missed your tight pussy,' he groans.

Carefully, so my body never touches anything but his cock, I clench and tighten my muscles around him and drag myself up and down that deliciously thick shaft. The nightmare falls away in pieces like leaves in autumn and makes me forget the tide of emotion that was aching to come out.

I whimper with pure pleasure and feel him get harder and bigger deep inside me. I know he will soon be at the point of no return. I feel his fingers move and locate my moist, swollen clit straining and protruding from its hood.

As his seed rushes upwards through his shaft he firmly grasps the tight bud between his fingers and squeezes it hard. The sudden furious sensation is so different from my gentle manipulations that it triggers my climax. I try not to buck too violently as the blissful spasms of my orgasm shake me from head to foot, but with his own climax upon him he instinctively forces more of his shaft into me, causing my buttocks to land on his thighs.

His groan is one of explosive ecstasy tempered by pain. For some time I hold him trapped within my body until our bodies are finally quiet. I remember once reading that the heart is like a tendril—it cannot flourish alone. It will always lean toward the nearest and loveliest thing it can twine itself with and cling to it. When I try to gently lift my body away he makes a sound of protest.

'What is it?' I whisper, thinking I have hurt him.

'I am so…' He hesitates. 'Proud of you.'

SEVENTEEN

A week after the fight, when only yellow bruises and unhealed ribs remain, we go to Jake's mother's house for lunch. She lives in a cottage with a charming English garden. English gardens are always best in spring but hers still looks good. There are hanging baskets of purple petunias by her front door. The door opens before we can knock and a surprisingly small woman, perhaps five feet three inches, with extraordinarily bright green eyes, smiles at us.

She kisses her son warmly on both his cheeks and formally extends her hand toward me. I am relieved by this show of formality. Her hands are small but strong—a gardener's hands. Jake introduces us.

'Nice to meet you, Lily,' she says. Her voice is soft but her accent is more pronounced than her son's.

'It's a pleasure to meet you, Mara,' I reply.

She withdraws her hand rather quickly and clasps it along with the other close to her chest.

'You better come in,' she says, and leads us into her living room. It is exactly as I expected it to be. As clean as two new pins with net curtains, family photos galore, and dainty china figurines on the windowsill.

'Take a seat,' she invites, and hovering uncertainly at the door asks if we would like something to drink.

'No, you sit down and I'll fix us all a drink. What will you have, Mother?'

I take the sofa and she perches on the end of a velour-covered Queen Anne chair. 'I'll have a sherry,' she says. I notice that her hands are tightly clenched in her lap.

'Lil?' Jake looks at me with a raised eyebrow.

'I'll have whatever you're having then.'

Jake walks to the carved armoire and opens it. One shelf holds an impressive selection of alcohol.

'So how did the two of you meet?' Mara probes.

I return my gaze to her. She is smiling politely, but her eyes are sharp. 'Shane introduced us,' I reply.

She frowns. 'Shane?'

'Yes, I was working as a dancer at Eden.'

'Dancer?'

Ah! Malice disguised as moral outrage. She just about stopped herself from crossing herself.

'She was,' Jake interrupts smoothly. 'She doesn't dance anymore.'

His mother turns to him. There is a puzzled, curious expression on her face. 'Oh!'

'Now she works for me.'

'Really?' she says softly, taking her glass of sherry from her son.

I have the urge to down the entire contents of my glass, but I don't. Instead I hold the glass in my hand and endure fifteen minutes of interrogation disguised as polite chat.

Finally, his mother stands. 'Please excuse me. I think lunch might be ready.' She disappears into the kitchen and I feel the tenseness in my shoulders go.

'I think she likes you,' Jake whispers.

'I think she doesn't,' I whisper back.

'I think she'll come around,' he consoles, and kisses me on the nose.

For some weird reason, his words touch me. I look into his eyes and he looks back and we are both so lost in each other's gaze that we don't hear his mother come back into the room.

She clears her throat and both of us turn to look at her. Her face is white and she seems shocked by something.

Even Jake notices. 'What's the matter, Mum?' he asks, standing up and going to her. He puts his arm around her narrow shoulders, making her appear smaller and quite fragile.

She shakes her head and smiles weakly. 'Someone walking over my grave.'

I stand, too, but I am conscious that she doesn't want me near her. The truth is that she can barely bring herself to look at me.

'Come on, lunch is ready,' she says briskly.

'Would you like some help?' I ask, knowing what the answer will be.

'Absolutely not. Everything is done.'

 116

So Jake and I take our seats at a dark wood dining table. The room faces her beautiful back garden full of flowers and fruit trees. His mother then disappears from the room and returns with a trolley.

'Be careful, the plates are hot,' she warns, setting our plates of a lamb chop, peas, carrots and potatoes in front of us. She places a basket of bread rolls and a gravy boat in the middle of the table and sits herself.

'May it do you good,' she says.

'May we all be together at the same time next year,' Jake says.

An expression of alarm crosses her face.

'Bon appétit,' I say.

Jake picks up his knife and fork.

His mother turns toward me. There is something in her eyes. For a second I think it is envy, the normal envy a mother feels for her son's chosen mate, and then I realize it is not envy. It is fear. She finds me terrifying. I am still staring at her in shock when her eyes slide away. She busies herself with tearing at a piece of bread, which she then lays down on the plate.

I turn to look at Jake. He has missed it all. He is cutting into a piece of meat. He catches my eyes as he carries it to his lips.

'What?' he asks

'Nothing.'

I look down at my plate. She wants to rub me out. Like a pencil mark that has been made in error. She cannot know who or what I really am,

but some instinct is driving her. Telling her I am not to be trusted. Not to be taken into her family.

The meal is a disaster. Both his mother and I hardly eat. As soon as Jake puts his knife and fork down, his mother turns to him. 'I need more ice. Will you get a bag from the freezer, Jake?'

'Sure.' Jake gets up and makes for the kitchen.

'Can you get it from the big freezer in the shed?' she says.

'Would you also like me to walk back very slowly?' he asks with a grin.

'That would be nice,' his mother replies, but there is no mischief in her voice. Only worry and trepidation.

As soon as the door closes she says, 'I've always preferred sketches to paintings. Paintings are closed, finished things that hide layers of lies. Sketches are the bones of what will be. They are more honest. They haven't learned to lie. What do you prefer?'

'If we are truly talking about sketches and paintings, then I prefer paintings. I know the finished product is a series of accidents, but I appreciate that the grand design of life allows accidents to become beautiful.'

She frowns. 'I want to have grandchildren. I want them to think of me as the old woman who wears shawls and silly hats and reads tea leaves. Are you the woman to give me that?'

I swallow. 'Look, Jake and I have just met. It's too early. It's not on the cards.'

'What do you want from my son, then?'

I shift uncomfortably. 'Did you ask this of all women he brought home?'

'He has never brought a woman home before.'

My mouth drops open.

'You haven't answered my question.'

'I don't want anything from your son. We're just in a relationship.'

'Liar,' she says very softly.

'What did you just call me?'

'You heard. You are a dangerously manipulative woman, Miss Hart. And I am here to tell you that I will never allow you to break this family, or my son for that matter.'

EIGHTEEN

As we fly into Las Vegas airport, I look out of my cabin window, and the sparkling city appears almost magically from the miles of desert surrounding it. The heat outside the airport hits me like a wall. We walk quickly toward a gleaming purple SUV, which is waiting outside for us. It is wonderfully cool inside.

'Purple?' I ask with a laugh.

'It's the Hard Rock touch,' Jake says.

We are in Las Vegas for the weekend, because I have never been, and when I told Jake that, he said, 'Well, you haven't lived until you've been on the Strip.'

The journey to the Strip is only about fifteen minutes. I gaze at the infamous street with wide eyes. It is an over the top, glamorous fantasy playground, almost like a giant Hollywood movie set with its miniatures of the Sphinx, pyramids, the Statue of Liberty and the Eiffel Tower. I even take a photo of the M & M store to show my mother.

I wonder what she will make of it. She once told me a shocking thing about the gorgeous black torch performer Lena Horne, who was allowed to stay at the Flamingo as long as she was not seen at the casino, restaurants or public areas. When she checked out, her bed sheets and towels were burned.

Over the massive, gold guitar door handles are the words: *When this house is rocking, don't bother knocking. Come on in.* And it really is rocking in there for Jake. There is no check-in for Jake and me. He is greeted by name by a smiling host and we are quickly and efficiently whisked past the awesome, fifty-five feet digital screen stretched behind the reception desk, straight to the elevator bank and up to the Provocateur penthouse suite.

The Provocateur suite is like no other hotel room I've been to.

We are greeted by walls covered in black vinyl embossed to look like crocodile skin in the foyer. In that deliberately darkened hallway there is a birdcage, large enough and strong enough to hold a grown man and a whipping cross! With handcuffs!

On our left, silhouettes of naked women start swaying provocatively in the shower as motion sensors pick up our movements. There can be no doubt that the design is fetish orientated and I turn to look at Jake.

Beyond the foyer are claret walls and sophisticated shiny black furniture and more dominatrix accessories. We are shown the heated plunge pool in the balcony and taken to the bedroom with three beds pushed together, presumably perfect for orgies. The other master bedroom has an enormous four-poster bed and a mirrored, trellised ceiling. The man shows us how to work the 3D projector system behind the bed to make it throw patterns and themes onto the walls.

At the flick of a button the shades come down, the lights dim and two women wantonly writhing are projected onto the bed. It is so over the top and creepy-crazy I start giggling. My laughter doesn't deter our host. We are taken to a secret vault full of toys, equipment and costumes for sex play.

When he is gone I go to stand by the ceiling-to-floor windows. The view is fabulous. Down below, the swimming pool is heaving with beautiful bodies on purple floats. I turn around to look at Jake.

'Like it?' he asks.

'Are you trying to tell me something Fifty Shades-ish?'

He laughs. 'No fucking way. I don't need to beat a woman to get my kicks. I just thought you'd enjoy this more than the Venetian. It's all Liberace style opulence, chocolate-covered strawberries and beluga caviar served by butlers with white gloves over there.'

'And you don't have to pay for any of this?'

He grins, at once boyish and delicious. 'Nope.'

'How come they treat you so good?'

He shrugs. 'My claim to fame is that I once lost a whole million at their baccarat table and they're hoping I'll repeat that lack of judgment,' he says dryly.

My eyes widen. 'One million? Dollars?'

'Yup. I used to be what they call a whale.'

'What's a whale?'

'At the lower end a high roller is someone who bets between a thousand to five thousand dollars a hand. A serious high roller would play upwards of five grand to about twenty, twenty-five thousand. A big high roller would spend between twenty-five and fifty thousand.' He stops and smiles. 'And then you have the whales. Whales start at seventy-five thousand dollars a hand.'

'And you were one of them?'

'I was. But now I only come two, maybe three times a year.'

'God!' It's hard for me to even think of anyone blowing that kind of money on the roll of a die.

'But I still get the eight o'clock reservation, the cabana, tickets for the best concerts in town, and... I get to be imaginative with my requests. So far the management has always said yes to everything I've asked for.'

'Wow! What kind of things are available?'

'Lunch on a yacht, a helicopter ride somewhere, a game of golf with Tiger Woods...'

'What have you asked for this time?'

He smiles slow and full of meaning. 'Lingerie. I have asked for the most expensive, most beautiful lingerie they can find.'

I can't help it, I flush hard. I can feel my cheeks flaming. 'You didn't.'

'I did. Go and have a look.'

For a few seconds I don't move. We just stare at each other. Then I turn around and go to the bedroom. At the door I stop and look around. He is watching me, his eyes unfathomable.

By the bedside I see the white box with a black design on it. I open it and it is full of whispers of baby blue lace: a half-cup bra, a thong, suspenders with white bows, and nude stockings. There is a card with a message to open the cupboard. I open the cupboard and gasp. A real cheongsam. Not the cheap thing that looks more like a Hong Kong waitress's uniform and with a dirty slit that runs all the way up to the crotch like I wore at the club, but the softest, most beautiful, pure white Chinese silk brocade. I run my fingers over the pretty little blue flowers. My grandmother would love this. I turn around and Jake is standing in the doorway.

'It is so very, very beautiful,' I whisper. I am so touched my voice shakes.

'Good. You can wear them all tonight.'

'Thank you.'

His eyes darken. 'Thank me later.'

'You look beautiful,' he tells me that night.

'So do you,' I say.

And he does. He looks good enough to eat. He is wearing a perfectly fitted black suit that totally showcases his great physique, an oyster gray silk shirt that is almost translucent, and polished black shoes. I have never seen him so subdued in his color scheme.

We go for an early dinner at Shanghai Lily. The food is exquisite. The last time I ate lobster that good I was in Singapore with my grandparents. There is even gold leaf on the food to gladden the hearts of the Asian high rollers since gold is considered a good luck charm.

We end up at the Shadow for drinks. I gaze in amazement at the giant backlit screens with the enlarged shadow of a woman dancing behind each one. It looks different from anything I have seen.

I drink a green cocktail and watch the bartenders, who are actually performers who throw bottles up into the air and catch those their colleagues have thrown. The atmosphere is young, fun and totally hip, and I turn my head, smiling, and catch Jake looking at me. The smile dies on my lips. His eyes are smoldering.

'What is it?' I ask.

His hand slides into the slit in my dress and up my thighs, parting them. 'I've always wanted to finger fuck you under a table in a public place.' One finger rubs suggestively against the string of my thong. He drops his voice to a whisper. 'Maybe because you won't be able to scream when you come, because everyone is watching.'

The green cocktail sings longingly in my veins as wetness seeps between my legs. My clit swells, begging for his touch. I put my drink down, suddenly daring and uninhibited. 'Knock yourself out,' I choke.

With a sensual growl he inserts one long finger into me.

I gasp.

His teeth flash in the dimness. 'Look at you. Always so wet and hot,' he says moving his finger in and out of me. 'Open your legs wider,' he invites, sliding the thumb of his other hand into my mouth. I catch it between my teeth and suck it. His thumb strokes in circles around my clit while his fingers curl inside me.

'We could get thrown out for this,' he whispers.

I release his thumb, my eyes glancing around furtively. It's dark and no one is looking. 'They wouldn't throw a whale out,' I choke.

'No, I guess not.'

'It will be a stern warning, though,' I mutter, wriggling and rubbing myself against his hand, loving the feel of his fingers inside me, his thumb working my clit.

'Damn, I love how filthy and greedy you are. How you'd let me do *anything* with you.'

He plunges his fingers deeper in and my muscles start clenching around them. 'I can't wait to get back to our room and see my big cock disappear between your sweet lips until I am balls deep in your mouth. And then I'd like to slide that saliva soaked cock, every fucking inch of it, into your poor little pussy. I am going to stretch her and fuck her until cum shoots out of her. And then I'm gonna suck her as she drips.'

'Oh Fuck! I'm coming,' I warn in a strangled gasp.

'Turn and look at me.'

I turn and look at him, my eyes wide, my face struggling to remain normal. Then the climax rips through me and I clench my teeth and shudder against his hand in an effort not to scream.

Afterwards, he puts his fingers into my mouth and makes me suck them.

NINETEEN

It is eleven o'clock on Saturday night, the lights are flashy, the rock ephemera is hip, and the gamblers are rocking, when we make our way through the casino toward the high limit gaming area called the Peacock Lounge, where once Jimi Hendrix's peacock vest was hung.

The high limit gaming area is a circular elevated platform off the main floor. It has its own cage and bar. It has obviously been arranged beforehand, so a roulette table has been wheeled in especially for Jake.

I look at Jake. 'Albert Einstein once said, "No one can win at roulette unless he steals money from the table while no one is looking."'

'If you look at roulette through the language of physics, then it is the universe in miniature, a whirling, glittering mix of forces all playing out their elegant tiny dances.'

'Very poetic.'

The croupier is an Asian girl. She smiles and nods. A man in a suit brings a tray of really cool psychedelic-colored chips and leaves them on the table in front of Jake.

Jake looks at them and smiles his thanks. He pushes five chips toward me. The chips have purple orange, yellow and green in them. Each one says five grand on it.

'I can't gamble this much money. I'll be devastated if I lose,' I say pushing the money back toward him.

He laughs and pushes it back to me. 'Keep it for now. Give it back to me later if you don't use it.'

He places a chip on Red and a chip on Even. The croupier starts rolling the wheel. The ivory ball spins on the outer ring. It leaves the outer track. No more bets.

'Thirty-three black,' she calls.

She places a marker on the 33 Black square and sweeps away his money. I swallow. Wow! That was ten thousand dollars gone in just seconds. When I look at him, his face is impassive.

This time he puts two chips on Red and two on Odd. The ball stops on 23 Red. I take a deep breath. He has won twenty thousand. People have begun to gather behind us to watch.

Jake repeats the same sequence and wins again.

A large suited man walks toward our table and stands unobtrusively at the side of it. His eyes are alert and watchful. Now more people come to watch. This time Jake puts five chips on Black and five on Even. A man puts his two chips next to Jake's.

The wheel turns—8 Black.

He has won a hundred thousand. I place my hand on his. I know how casinos work. The smart player never stays. The longer you stay, the more unlikely you will walk away with anything. 'Shouldn't you stop now? You've won so much.'

He looks at me, a strange expression on his face. 'Remember what I told you, Lil? I'm lucky. I'm always lucky.'

He puts the entire winnings, a hundred thousand dollars, on 34 Red. The crowd behind us gasps. It's straight up betting. Pays thirty-five to one but the chances of winning are so small.

I touch his sleeve, my eyes confused. I can't understand what he is up to. Why abandon his earlier winning and more careful strategy? 'Why?'

'Lucky at games and unlucky in love. If I win then I am unlucky in love and if I lose it means I am lucky in love. What do you say, Lil? Is a hundred thousand dollars worth it?'

The woman spins the wheel. I stare at the wheel in bewilderment. Then I put my chips behind his.

'No more bets,' the woman says.

I look at his face and he is staring at me, totally unperturbed. He has no interest in the outcome of his bet. There is a disappointed hush. Hazily, I hear the words, 'Fourteen Red.' All the chips are swept away.

'They don't call it the Strip for nothing,' he murmurs. He is strangely calm.

He slips his hand into his pocket and comes up with a small velvet box. I stare at it in shock. He opens the box.

A huge, glittering diamond solitaire stares back at me. I am shaken out of my daze by a commotion at my side. I lift my head and see the award-winning Blue Man Group! Their shiny blue painted heads bob and they widen their eyes and start to turn placards around that read:

Will
You
Marry
Me,
Lily
Hart?

My mouth drops open. The people around us 'Oh,' and 'Ah.' What the hell is going on? The whole thing is so unreal I almost can't believe my eyes. I glance at Jake and he is grinning at me. The men start pantomiming beating hearts in their own inimitable way. They then produce a bottle of Kristal champagne and pop that open. Two flutes appear from somewhere and get filled. One is handed to me. Utterly bemused I take it and turn toward Jake. My mind is a total blank.

'Will you?' Jake asks softly.

'Was this your high roller request?' I whisper.

'Part of it. It's not finished yet.'

My brain can't get into gear. The cocktails have made it sluggish. It has all happened so fast. I don't know what I would have done in different circumstances, but with no time for thought or reflection, this moment seems like the most beautiful thing anyone has ever done for me. It is the most romantic and certainly the most dramatic. And all these people are waiting for me to say yes.

Caught in the moment my voice is a whisper. 'Yes. Yes, I will.'

With a triumphant smile he slips the ring onto my finger. It is a perfect fit and the crowd starts clapping and congratulating us.

'Come,' he says, and we go out to the pool area. It has been turned into a magical wonderland full of flowers, balloons and lights. There is an altar and a priest is waiting for us.

'What the hell?' People are clapping, laughing, and cheering us on.

'Feel like becoming my wife tonight?'

'Tonight?' I squeak. 'It's nearly midnight.'

'Why not? This is Las Vegas—the land of dreams and twenty-four hour marriage ceremonies.'

I suddenly remember Mills and what he would say. Shit. What the fuck am I doing? This is not part of the plan. A feeling of uneasiness slithers down my spine, cold and restless. I want to say, 'We should wait. This is all too fast,' but I am unable to. He has gone to so much trouble and everyone is looking at me with a mixture of envy and awe. I look up at him.

A warm gust of wind ripples through his hair, as if it is teasing fingers. He looks down at me, reckless and intense. I stare at him, mesmerized. He is as gorgeous as a technicolor dream. I am the luckiest girl here.

I open my mouth and words tumble out. 'Yes, I'll marry you.'

With a smile the priest announces, 'You may kiss your bride.'

As if in a dream I watch Jake drift closer, his eyes flashing, triumphant. Daring me? Daring me to what? Then I feel his mouth come down on me and drown out every thought in my head. My legs go weak. I'm married. I'm married to Jake Eden. Without my parents or grandmother. A sharp guilt pierces me.

What the hell have I done?

But everybody is shouting. There is glitter and noise. A photographer and videographer appear. Hotel staff are congratulating us. And there is a pink cake to cut. A small piece is put into my

mouth. It feels soft, but I don't taste it. It must have been sweet.

Then Jake is pulling me by the hand. He pulls me into the elevator. I look up at him, still dazed, unable to believe: I'm married. We just got married. In the confines of the lift I can't look into his eyes. I look down at my ring. Wow! I'm married. I'm *really* married. A tendril of happiness touches my heart.

We start kissing in the lift. He pulls me out and we stumble through the doors, our lips glued. Suddenly he breaks away and, putting his hand under my knees, lifts me up.

'What are you doing?'

'Carrying you over the threshold.'

I laugh. Who would ever have thought I could be so carefree and happy again? He carries me past that dim foyer and puts me down in the living room with its scarlet walls.

'Show me what's underneath the dress, Mrs. Eden.'

I am suddenly shy. I bite my lip. He propels me to the middle of the room and drops himself onto the black couch. He leans back, his legs wide open, relaxed, wanting a show.

I undo the clasp on the high neck and pull down the zip. The dress shimmers all the way down to the floor, leaving me standing in my underwear, suspenders, stockings and high heels. I step away from my dress and slowly sway up to him. Once in front of him I stand with my legs apart. He lets his gaze travel slowly over my body.

'Turn around and show me your bum,' he says.

Intoxicated by the hunger in his eyes, I turn around and jut my bottom out provocatively. I look back and see his eyes rush to my crotch where the pale blue string of my thong is caught between my sex lips. Without removing his eyes from me, he takes his jacket off and pulls his shirt out of his trousers.

I turn back around and, with my hands behind my back, fiddle with my bra strap, while I slide my tongue over my bottom lip. I know that always drives him crazy.

'Go on,' he mutters, unbuttoning his shirt.

I take the bra off.

'Jesus, you're so fucking sexy.' The pupils of his eyes are dilated and huge.

'What do you want off next?' I sound all breathy and bimbo-ish.

'That bit of string stuck to your pussy.'

I laugh giddily.

His expression doesn't change. He stares as if bewitched. I used to wonder what it would be like to be with someone who made me feel so desired, so wanted, so special. Now I know. I don't know what the future holds. But it can never take this moment away from me.

I take it off and holding it in my hand, scandalize myself by bringing it to my nose and smelling the string.

 135

He catches his breath and standing up steps out of his trousers and boxers. He runs his hand along the curve of my buttocks. My skin burns faintly at his touch.

'So slender,' he murmurs, the sound warm and intimate. Then he bends down and swipes his velvety tongue slowly and tantalizingly along the crack. 'And as sweet as sin,' he whispers. He moves upwards, flicks his tongue on the rim of my ear, catches the lobe between his teeth, and suddenly nips me. My stomach curls and I moan.

He catches my waist and spins me around, his gaze adoring. I slide my wrists around his neck and press my body invitingly against his hardness. I am desperate to feel my breasts crushed against the dark hair on his chest and his hot, wet mouth on them. I want his hands to spread my open thighs and gorge himself on the swollen whorls of flesh there.

But he doesn't.

Instead, he pulls me toward the ceiling-to-floor windows. My palms connect with the cold surface and I see the panoramic view of the city glittering with neon lights surrounded by miles of dark desert. I feel him tilt my hips up toward him, and enter me in a fierce thrust. And I see my shining reflection open its mouth in a startled gasp.

'You like it rough?'

'Yes.'

He thrusts again, harder. 'Like this?'

'Yes,' I gasp.

I feel him pull apart my buttocks and the next thrust is so hard and so deep that my body jerks like a puppet. My eyes swivel upwards, dimly noticing the stars like jewels in the soft blackness of the night sky. A thought hits me: All that I need is to be his. Like this. Forever.

'Nobody has taken you so hard before, have they?'

'No.'

'Nobody ever will again, will they?'

'No,' I moan.

'Because this is all mine. I own all of this now, don't I?'

'Yes, yes, yes.'

His finger drums relentlessly at the side of my clit. The sensation causes a rush of aching warmth to start flooding my body. He keeps up the thrusts and the drumming until I explode and splinter into a thousand pieces. I am slumped against the glass when I feel him climax. He comes with a fierce bark of humorless laughter.

I rest against the glass panting, slowly returning.

'Do you know,' he whispers close to my ear, his voice sensation soaked, lazy. 'I dreamed about you.'

'Really,' I murmur. I am pleasantly satiated. I want to keep him inside me forever.

'Don't you want to know what I dreamed?'

'What did you dream?' My voice is lazy, playful.

 137

'We went out, we had dinner, we had sex... And then you betrayed me.'

I freeze, the blood congealing in my veins. He saw me coming!

In the glass I see his face gleaming dimly, as insubstantial as a ghost. It is a moment so simple, but so heightened because of that very simplicity. Life rarely offers such moments of profound clarity. It is as if I have trained for years for this moment. I see its preciousness glittering like a cornered rat's eyes. Kill or be killed. Hesitating is to make the second choice.

I whisk around, eyes wide, clumsy and unsteady in my heels.

His face is tight as a carved marble bust. The glass behind my back is shockingly cold and the silence between us is leaden. Suddenly I feel the way Eve must have felt, so naked, so exposed, and so *fucking* guilty.

He stands a foot away from me, touching distance, and simply looks at me. As if he is looking at a piece of modern art and trying to figure out what the artist intended to say with his senseless splashes of color. I try to imagine what he must be seeing.

After you cut all the bullshit about making the world a safer place and my gnawing shame that I was not there for Luke when he needed me, what is left? A sad, lonely, despicable bitch, who tried to use her body to get some information and failed miserably.

I open my mouth and, honestly, I don't know what I was planning to say, but he lays a silencing finger across my lips.

'Don't lie, baby,' he advises softly.

I shake my head. I can feel the tears gathering at the backs of my eyes. I blink hard and fast. He takes his hand away.

'Did you tell them about the sixteenth?'

Dismay curves my spine. I close my eyes and nod.

I hear him sigh softly.

I open my eyes and he is looking at me with an expression so sad that I want to press my body against his and hold him, but I can't. I couldn't bear it if he pushed me away. God! It had seemed so real only a moment ago and yet it was all only a mirage. I feel my body trembling.

'When did you find out?' My voice is just a string.

'Maybe I always knew. I just didn't want to believe it.'

'How?' A part of me wants to know where I went wrong.

One corner of his lips twists. 'Everything about you was off. You were too clean to be a runaway. And a runaway who has never let a man come inside her before? And there is one more thing that you might want to reconsider before you go back to being an undercover asset. You talk in your sleep.'

'I do?' I say hoarsely.

'That time when you were attacked you said, "Get Crystal Jake." I knew then for sure. No one calls me that anymore.'

'So you admit dealing in drugs?'

He frowns. 'How have I just admitted to dealing in drugs?'

'Crystal Jake because you were selling crystal meth.'

'Is that what they told you?' He grasped his crystal chain and tugged hard at it. It broke, sending sparkling crystals flying across the room, hitting the floor. With his other hand he took my hand, opened my palm, put in what was left in his fist and closed my hand. 'That is why I was called Crystal Jake. I have *never* sold hard drugs.'

My gaze moves from my closed fist up to his eyes. I don't know whether to believe him, but he has never lied to me, and it is true that the whole time I have been with him I have not seen any evidence of drug usage or dealing either at Eden or on a personal level.

I stare at him as I have never seen him before. As the man I am in love with. All this while I have been pretending—to him and to myself—that I'm not. But I love him. I love this gangster who seems more honest and sincere than a priest. Other than the bed covered in used money I have no evidence that he is a gangster anyway.

He walks away from me and begins to dress. I stand at the glass, naked and frozen, all kinds of thoughts churning through my mind. He comes back fully dressed and looks at me. There is contempt in his eyes.

'Why did you marry me if you knew?'

'So that no one will be able to force you to testify against me. If you do, it will be because you want to.'

My mouth drops open. For some reason his answer is painful on a shocking level. 'How could you marry me for that reason?'

'How could you show me your naked body and keep your heart covered? Tell them the next time they want another swipe at me it might be an idea not to send such a rookie.' He looks at me with hard, derisive eyes. 'Enjoy your wedding night, Mrs. Eden.'

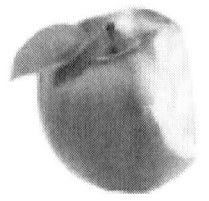

Oh
The damage is done
So I guess I be leavin'
—Cry me a River, Justin Timberlake

TWENTY

For a long time I stand staring at the closed door. A part of me is horrified, but a part of me that I have hidden for so long is strangely elated that the lie is finally out in the open. I don't have to pretend anymore. Nude, I walk to the fully stocked bar. I open a bottle of whiskey and drink it straight from the bottle. It glugs down my throat, burning all the way down. I cough and pat my chest. The sound is loud in the empty suite.

Tears press against my eyelids. I feel alone, helpless, and so incredibly lost. I have failed miserably. And I have only myself to blame. I pick up the cheongsam from the floor, and carefully hang it in the closet. It is my wedding dress. I let my fingers skim the silky material one last time. The chambermaid will find it. It will be a nice treat for her. Then I go into the bathroom and, avoiding my reflection, dress in my own clothes.

Then I sit on the bed and wait for him. I am convinced he will come back through the door. He could not have just walked out on me. But an hour later I know he is not coming back. Reality hits. The truth is like switching on a light. All this time I had thought my eyes were accustomed to the dark. I had made out shapes from the shadows and guessed their names.

But it was a lie.

He knew I was an undercover cop the whole time and he was only pretending. Everything we had was a lie. Maybe the lust was real, but what is lust but dust without love? All that time he knew. I think of all the people and the planning that must have gone into hiring The Blue Man Group, the lavish wedding. He had lost all that money on purpose. To keep the invisible balance ledger between him and the casino straight.

The breath comes out of me in a rush. Now I understand why he asked for this particular suite. The Provocateur suite.

The message was there for me to see. Only I was too proud of my own ability to deceive and too blinded by my own feelings. I feel tears prickling at the backs of my eyes. No, I won't give in now. I know what happens when I give in to grief. It takes over. I become a total wreck. No more introspection. I can't stay here anymore.

My instructions are very clear in the event that my cover is ever blown.

I pick up the phone, make flight reservations. Then I pack my bag quickly and with little fuss. There is not much to pack, anyway. I open my purse and take out the black plastic chip. Worthless here, but worth ten thousand dollars at Eden.

I remember that sweltering night as if it happened yesterday. How exciting it had all been

144

then. How naïve I was to give in to temptation and not think it would scar me for life. I put the chip on the pillow on his side of the bed. I don't know why I bother after the cavalier way he lost all that money in the casino earlier, but I know I can't keep it. *At the end of the operation you will ditch all the physical trappings of your undercover alter ego, the hair, the clothes, the people you have befriended, and return to your own normal world.*

Then I go out to the lounge to sit and wait. I know I am a wreck waiting to happen, but at this moment I feel strangely detached and calm. It is simple, I tell myself. My cover is blown. I am not the first undercover cop it has happened to. It has happened many times. I will simply report back and they will assign me somewhere else. Somewhere I can go to lick my wounds. Where there won't be a Jake Eden I will fall in love with and suffer over.

I look at the time. I call reception and order a cab. In thirty minutes the cab will arrive and take me to the airport. I will be fine. Of course I will be fine.

A small voice says, 'Don't run away. Stay. Fight for your man.'

But he is not my man. He is nobody's man. He was pretending the whole time. I have been silly. I allowed myself to fall in love. It is not so despicable. Other cops have done it. Over the course of years of being undercover some have married their targets and even had children with them. I am not so despicable.

I stand. I can't stay in this room any longer. I will wait in reception downstairs. I pick up my luggage, take one last look at the opulence around me, and walk resolutely to the door.

I open it and stop dead in my tracks. My luggage falls from my disbelieving hands.

Jake Eden is sitting sprawled out in the corridor. His back is resting against the opposite wall and beside him is an empty bottle of Scotch. He has another in his right hand, which is already half empty. He looks up, trying to hold his lids open.

'Leaving so soon?' he slurs.

Last part out sooner than you think... ☺

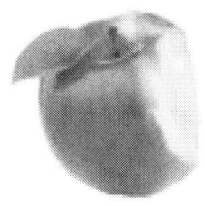

Want To Leave A Review?

No matter how short it may be, it is precious.
Please use these links:

United States
http://www.amazon.com/dp/B00U1F03RE

United Kingdom
http://www.amazon.co.uk/gp/product/B00
U1F03RE

Canada
http://www.amazon.ca/gp/product/B00U1
F03RE

Australia
http://www.amazon.com.au/gp/product/B0
0U1F03RE

Coming Next:

Want to know what the Billionaire Banker did to his woman?

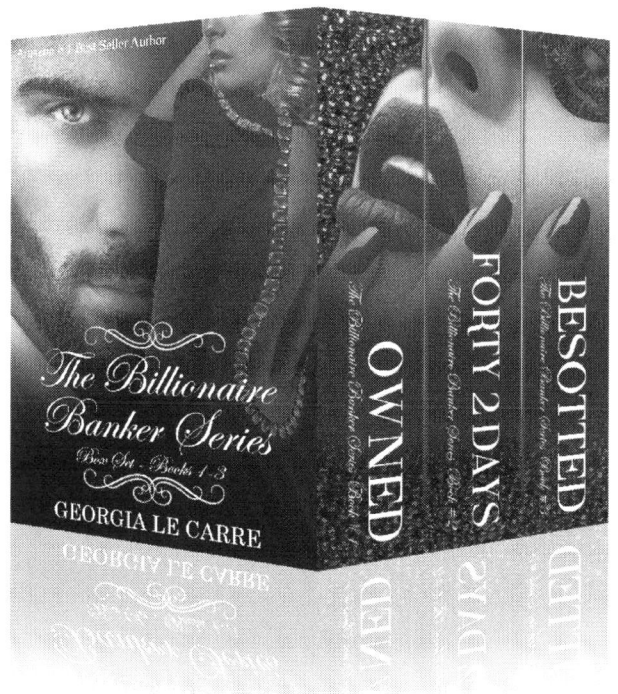

The Billionaire Banker Series

http://www.amazon.com/dp/B00M08LS6A

http://www.amazon.co.uk/dp/B00M08LS6A

http://www.amazon.com.au/gp/product/B00M08LS6A

http://www.amazon.ca/gp/product/B00M08LS6A

The Billionaire Banker Series

Book One

GEORGIA LE CARRE

You aren't wealthy until you have something money can't buy.

—Garth Brooks

One

Blake Law Barrington

I drop a cube of sugar into the creamy face of my espresso, stir it, and glance at my platinum Greubel Forsey Tourbillion, acquired at Christie's Important Watches auction last autumn for a cool half a million dollars.

Eight minutes past eight.

I have a party to go to tonight, but I'm giving it a miss. It's been a long day, I am tired, I have to be in New York early tomorrow morning, and it will be one of those incomprehensibly dreary affairs. I take a sip—superb coffee—and return the tiny cup to its white rim.

Summoning a waiter for the check, I sense the activity level in the room take a sudden hike. Automatically, I lift my eyes to where all the other eyes, mostly male and devouring, have veered to. Of course. A girl. In a cheap, orange dress and lap dancer's six-inch high plastic platforms.

You're looking for love in all the wrong places, honey.

A waiter in a burgundy waistcoat bearing the bill has silently materialized at my side. Not taking my eyes off the girl—despite the impossible shoes she has a good walk, sexy—I order myself a whiskey. The waiter slinks away after a right-away-sir nod, and I lean back into the plush chair to watch the show.

It is one of those swanky restaurants where there are transparent black voile curtains hung between the tables and discreet fans to tease and agitate the gauzy material. Three curtains away she stands, minus the shoes, perhaps five feet five or six inches tall. She has the same body type as Lady Gaga, girlishly narrow with fine delicate limbs. Her skin is the color of thick cream. Beautiful mouth. My eyes travel from the waist-length curtain of jet-black hair to the swelling curve of her breasts and hips, and down her shapely legs.

Very nice, but...

At twenty-nine, I am already jaded. Though I watch her with the same speculation of all the other men in the room she is a toy that no longer holds any real excitement for me. I do not need to meet her to *know* her. I have had hundreds like her—hot, greedy pussies and cold, cold hearts. It is always the same. Each one hiding talons of steely ambition that hook into my flesh minutes after they rise like resurrected phoenixes from a night in my bed. Safe to say I have realized the error of my ways.

Still....

Something about her *has* aroused my attention.

She comes further into the room and even the billowing layers of curtains cannot conceal her great beauty or youth. Certainly she is far too young for her dining companion who has just barged in with all the grace of a retired rugby player. I recognize his swollen head instantly. Rupert Lothian. An over-privileged, nerve gratingly colossal ass. He is one of the bank's high profile private customers. The bank never does business with anyone they do not check out first and his report was sickening.

Curious. What could someone so fresh-faced and beautiful be doing with one so noted for ugly games? And they are ugly games that Lothian plays.

I watch three waiters head off towards them and the fluid, elegantly choreographed dance they perform to seat and hand them their menus. Now I have her only in profile. She has put the menu on the table and is sitting ramrod-straight with her hands tightly clasped in her lap. She crosses and uncrosses her legs nervously.

Unbidden, an image pops into my head. It is as alive and wicked as only an image can be. Those long, fine legs entangled in silky sheets. I stare helplessly as she pulls away the sheets, turns that fabulous mouth into a red O, and deliberately opens her legs to expose her sex to me. I see it clearly. A juicy, swollen fruit that my tongue wants to explore! I sit forward abruptly.

Fuck.

I thought I had passed the season of fantasizing about having sex with strangers. I reach for my whiskey and shoot it. From the corner of my eyes I see a waiter discreetly whisper something to Lothian. He rises with all the pomposity he can muster and leaves with the waiter.

I transfer my attention to the girl again. She has collapsed backwards into the chair. Her shoulders sag and her relief is obvious. She stares moodily at the tablecloth, fiddles with her purse and frowns. Then, she seems to visibly force herself away from whatever thoughts troubled her, and lets her glance wander idly around the room until her truly spectacular eyes—I have never seen anything like them before—collide with my unwavering stare. And through the gently shifting black gauze my breath is suddenly punched out of my body, and I am seized by an unthinking, irresistible call to hunt. To possess.

To *own* her.

Two

Lana Bloom

It can have been only seconds, but it seems like ages that I am held locked and hypnotized by the stranger's insolent eyes. When I recall it later I will remember how startlingly white his shirt had been against his tanned throat, and swear that even the air between us had shimmered. Strange too how all the background sounds of cutlery, voices and laughter had faded into nothing. It was as if I had wandered into a strange and compelling universe where there was no one else but me and that devilishly handsome man.

But in this universe I am prey.

The powerful spell is broken when he raises his glass in an ironic salute. Hurriedly, I tear my gaze away, but my thin façade of poise is completely shattered. Hot blood is rushing up into my neck and cheeks; and my heart is racing like a mad thing.

What the hell just happened?

I can still feel his gaze like a burning tingle on my skin. To hide, I bend my head and let my hair fall forward. But the desire to dare another look is so immense it shocks me. I have never experienced such an instant and physical attraction before.

With broad shoulders, a deep tan, smoldering eyes, a strong jaw, and straight-out-of-bed, vogue-cool, catwalk hair that flops onto his forehead, he looks like one of those totally hot and brooding Abercrombie and Fitch models, only more savage and fierce.

Devastatingly more.

But I am not here to flirt with drop dead gorgeous strangers, or to find a man for myself. I press my fingers against my flaming cheeks, and force myself to calm down. All my concentration must go into getting Rupert to agree to my proposal. He is my last hope.

My only hope.

Nothing could ever be more important than my reason for being there with such a man as him. I look miserably towards the tall doors where he has gone. This cold, pillared place of opulence is where rich people come to eat. A waiter wearing white gloves comes through the doors bearing a covered tray. I feel out of my depth. The orange dress is itchy and prickly and I long to scratch several places on my body. Then there are the butterflies flapping dementedly inside my stomach.

Don't ruin this, I tell myself angrily. You've come this far. Nervously, to regain my composure, I press my lips together and firmly push the sarcastically curving mouth out of my mind. I must concentrate on the horrible task ahead. But those insolent eyes, they will not go. So I bring to mind my mother's thin, sad face, and suddenly the stranger's eyes are magically gone. I straighten my back. Prepare myself.

I will not fail.

Rupert, having met whomever he had gone to meet, is weaving his way back to me and when our eyes touch I flash him a brilliant smile. I will not fail. He smiles back triumphantly, and coming around to my side drops me a quick kiss, before slumping heavily into his seat. I have to stop myself from reaching up to wipe my mouth.

I stare at him. He seems transformed. Expansive, almost jolly.

'That's one deal that came in the nick of time. As if the heavens have decided that I deserve you.' The way he says it almost makes me flinch with horror.

'Lucky me,' I say softly, flirtatiously, surprising myself. I tell myself I am playing a part. One that I can vanish into and emerge from unscathed, but I know it is not true. There will be repercussions and consequences.

He smiles nastily. He knows I do not fancy him, but that is part of the thrill. Taking what does not want to be taken.

'Well then,' he says. 'Don't be coy, let's hear it. How much are you going to cost me?'

I take a deep breath. A bull this large can only be taken by the horns. 'Fifty thousand pounds.'

His dirty blond eyebrows shoot upwards, but his voice is mild. 'Not exactly cheap.' His lips thin. 'What do I get for my money?'

We are both startled out of our conversation by a deep, curt voice.

'Rupert.'

'Mr. Barrington,' Rupert gasps, and literally flies to his feet. 'What an unexpected pleasure,' he croons obsequiously. I drop my head with searing shame. It is the stranger. He has heard me sell myself.

'I don't believe I've had the pleasure of your companion's acquaintance,' he says. His voice is an intriguing combination of velvet and husk.

'Blake Law Barrington, Lana Bloom, Lana Bloom, Blake Law Barrington.'

I look up then, a long way up—he is definitely over six feet, maybe six two or three—to meet his stormy-gray stare. I search them for disgust, but they are carefully veiled, impenetrable pits of mystery. Perhaps, he has not heard me sell myself, after all. I begin to tremble. My body knows something I do not. He is dangerous to me in a way I cannot yet conceive.

'Hello, Lana.'

'Hi,' I reply. My voice sounds tiny. Like a child that has been told to greet an adult.

He puts his hand out, and after a perceptible hesitation, I put mine into it. His hand is large and warm, and his clasp firm and safe, but I snatch mine away as if burnt. He breaks his gaze briefly to glance at Rupert.

'There is a party tonight at Lord Jakie's,' he says before those darkly fringed eyes return to me again. Inscrutable as ever. 'Would you like to come as my guests?' It is as if he is addressing only me. It sends delicious shivers up and down my spine. Confused, by the unfamiliar sensations I tear my eyes away from him and look at Rupert.

Rupert's eyebrows are almost in his hairline. 'Lord Jakie?' he repeats. There is unconcealed delight in his face. He seems a man who has found a bottle of rare wine in his own humble cellar. 'That's terribly kind of you, Mr. Barrington. Terribly kind. Of course, we'd love to,' he accepts for both of us.

'Good. I'll leave your names at the door. See you there.' He nods at me and I register the impression that he is obsessively clean and controlled. There is no mess in this man's life. A place for everything and everything in its place. Then he is gone.

Rupert and I watch him walk away. He has the stride of a supremely confident man. Rupert turns to face me again; his face is mean and at odds to his words. 'Well, well,' he drawls, 'You must be my lucky charm.'

'Why?'

'First, I get the deal I've been after for the last year and a half, then the great man not only deigns to speak to me, but invites me to a party thrown by the crème de la crème of high society.'

'Who is he?'

'He, my dear, is the next generation of arguably the richest family in the world.'

'*The* Barringtons?' I whisper, shocked.

'He even smells of old money and establishment, doesn't he?' Rupert says, and neighs loudly at his own joke. Rupert himself smells like grated lemon peel. The citrusy scent reminds me of Fairy washing up liquid.

A waiter appears to ask what we would like to drink.

'We'll have your finest house champagne,' Rupert booms. He winks at me. 'We're celebrating.'

A bottle and ice bucket arrive with flourish. The only time I have drunk champagne is when Billie and I dressed up to the nines and presented ourselves as bride and bridesmaid to be, at the Ritz. We pretended I was about to drop forty thousand pounds into their coffers by cutting my wedding cake there. We quaffed half a bottle of champagne and a whole tray of canapés while being shown around the different function rooms. Afterwards, Billie thanked them nicely and said we would be in touch. How we had laughed on the bus journey back.

I watch as the waiter expertly extracts the cork with a quiet hiss. Another waiter in a black jacket reels off the specials for the night and asks us if we are ready to order.

Rupert looks at me. 'The beef on the bone here is very good.'

I smile weakly. 'I guess I'll just have whatever you're having.'

'I'm actually having steak tartare.'

'Then I'll have the same.'

He looks at the waiter. 'A dozen oysters to start then steak tartare and side orders of vegetables and mashed potatoes.'

'I'm not really hungry. No starter for me,' I say quickly.

When the waiter is gone, he raises his glass. 'To us.'

'To us,' I repeat softly. The words stick in my throat.

I take a small sip and taste nothing, so I put the glass on the table and look at my hands blankly. I have to find something interesting to say.

'You have very beautiful skin,' he says softly. 'It was the first thing I noticed about you. Does it...mark very easily?'

'Yes,' I admit warily.

'I knew it,' he boasts with a sniff. 'I am a connoisseur of skin. I love the taste and the touch of skin. I can already imagine the taste of yours. A skin of wine.' He eyes me greedily over the rim of his glass.

I have been trying my best not to look at the dandruff flakes that liberally dust the shoulders

of his pin-striped suit, but with that last remark he has tossed his head and a flurry of motes have floated off his head and fallen onto the pristine tablecloth. My eyes have helplessly followed their progress. I look up to find him looking at me speculatively.

'What will I be getting for my money?' His voice is suddenly cold and hard.

I blink. It is all wrong. I shouldn't be here. In this dress, or shoes, sitting in front of this obscene piece of filth hiding behind his handmade shirt, gold cufflinks and plummy, upper class accent. This man degrades and offends me simply by looking at me. I wish myself somewhere else, but I am here. All my credit cards are maxed out. Two banks have impolitely turned me down and there is nothing else to do, but be here in this dress and these slutty shoes…

My stomach in knots, I smile in what I hope is a seductive way. 'What would you like for your money?'

'Forget what I would like for the moment. What are you selling?' His eyes are spiteful in a way I cannot understand.

'Me, I guess.'

That makes him snort with cruel laughter. 'You are an extraordinarily beautiful girl, but to be honest I can get five first class supermodels right off the runway for that asking price. What makes you think you're worth that kind of money?'

 163

I take a deep breath. Here goes. 'I'm a virgin.'

He stops laughing. A suspicious speculative look enters his pale blue eyes. 'How old are you?'

'Twenty.' Well, I will be in two months' time.

He frowns. 'And you say you're still a virgin?'

'Yes.'

'Saving yourself up for someone special, were you?' His tone is annoying.

'Does it matter?' My nails bite into my clenched fists.

His eyes glitter. 'No, I suppose not.' He pauses. 'How do I know you're not lying?'

I swallow hard. The taste of my humiliation is bitter. 'I'll undergo any medical tests you require me to.'

He laughs. 'No need. No need,' he dismisses genially. 'Blood on the sheets will be enough for me.'

The way he says blood makes my blood run cold.

'Are all orifices up for sale?'

Oh! the brutality of the man. Something dies inside me, but I keep the image of my mother in my mind, and my voice is clear and strong. 'Yes.'

'So all that is left is to renegotiate the price?'

I have to stop myself from recoiling. I know now that I have committed two out of the nine sorts of behaviors my mother has warned me are considered contemptible and base. I have expected generosity from a miser and I have revealed my need to my enemy. 'The price is not negotiable.'

His gaze sweeps meaningfully to my champagne glass. 'Shall we give this party a go first and bargain later, when you are in a...better mood?'

I understand his thinking. He thinks he can drive the price down when I am drunk. 'The price is not negotiable,' I say firmly. 'And will have to be paid up front.'

He smiles smarmily. 'I'm sure we'll come to some agreement that we will both be happy with.'

I frown. I have been naïve. My plan is sketchy and has no provisions for a sharp punter or price negotiations. I heard through the office grapevine where I worked as temporary secretary that my boss was one of those men who are prepared to pay ten thousand pounds a pop for his pleasure and often, but I had never imagined he would reduce me to bargaining.

While Rupert stuffs himself with cheese and biscuits I excuse myself and go to the Ladies. There is another woman standing at the mirror. She glances at me with a mixture of surprise and disgust. I wait until she leaves, then I call my mother.

'Hi, Mum.'

'Where are you, Lana?'

'I'm still at the restaurant.'

'What time will you be coming home?'

'I'll be late. I've been invited to a party.'

'A party,' my mother repeats worriedly. 'Where?'

'I don't know the address. Somewhere in London.'

'How will you get home?' A wire of panic has crept into her voice.

I sigh gently. I have almost never left my mother alone at night; consequently she is now a bundle of jittery nerves. 'I have a ride, Mum. Just don't wait up for me, OK?'

'All right. Be careful, won't you?'

'Nothing is going to happen to me.'

'Yes, yes,' she says, but she sounds distracted and unhappy.

'How are you feeling, Mum?'

'Good.'

'Goodnight, then. I'll see you in the morning.'

'Lana?'

'Yeah.'

'I love you very much.'

'Me too, Mum. Me too.'

I flip my phone shut with a snap. I no longer feel cheap or obscene, but strong and sure. There is nothing Rupert can do that can degrade me. I will have that money no matter what.

I look at myself in the mirror. No need for lipstick as I have hardly eaten—just watching Rupert gurgle down the oysters made me feel quite sick, and how was I to know steak tartare was ground raw meat. For a moment I think again of that sinfully sophisticated man, his eyes edged with experience and mystery, his lips twisted with sensuality, and I am suddenly overcome by a strong desire to press my body against his hard length. But he is gone and I am here.

I return my phone to my purse and go out to meet my fate.

End of Sample

To receive news of my latest releases &
exclusive giveaways, click here.

http://bit.ly/10e9WdE

Don't forget I **LOVE** hearing from readers
so do come and say hello here:

https://www.facebook.com/georgia.lecarre

xx Georgia

17406244R00106

Printed in Great Britain
by Amazon